Honeymoon

Honeymoon

A Novel

by

Rebecca Kavaler

H \S

HAMILTON STONE EDITIONS

Library of Congress Cataloging-in-Publication Data

Kavaler, Rebecca.
Honeymoon / by Rebecca Kavaler.
    p. cm.
ISBN 978-0-9801786-5-4 (alk. paper)
1.   Newlyweds—Fiction. 2. Cults—Fiction. I. Title.

PS3568.A76M68 2008
813'.54—dc22
2008002944

Cover by Lou Robinson

H \S

HAMILTON STONE EDITIONS
P.O. Box 43, Maplewood, New Jersey 07040

Honeymoon

In the Beginning

Their second love-making was far more satisfying than the anxious initial coupling. It's like being interviewed for a job, Jane thought: no matter how often you've been accepted, the fear of not meeting the requirements is as strong as it was that first time. Now resting flank to flank, they were making conversational forays into each other's lives but still keeping to the border marches of parents and siblings and mutual friends (my parents are divorced, Jane said; my mother is dead, Boone capped her).

"How long have you known Andrea?"

"Who's Andrea?" Boone asked incuriously.

"What do you mean, who's Andrea? It was at her party we met."

But he had never met Andrea, he had been dragged to that party by a friend just divorced, who, after accepting every invitation that came his way, at the last minute chickened out. "Nick Fedor—the guy you were talking to when I came over. You might say I dragged *him* —he wouldn't go unless I came along to provide moral support."

"Balding men shouldn't wear pony tails," Jane said dogmatically. But her thoughts were elsewhere. "And really, a man asking for moral support! For a party, I mean. Most women are uncomfortable"—terrified, was what she meant—"entering a roomful of strangers, but I always thought that kind of feeling was gender-based."

Boone was not about to destroy her illusions. "Oh well, Nick is still feeling a little weak in the knees. It was a very painful divorce, you know."

"Is there any other kind?" Jane asked. For one who laid claim to being single, never married, the bitterness took him by surprise. Then he remembered the parents.

"On the other hand, marriage can be painful too," Boone said, thinking of his own parents, although not until death did them part had he any inkling of their pain.

Jane agreed, almost dreamily. "As institutions go, it's the pits. It needs re-inventing a hell of a lot more than government does."

"Oh, there's plenty of that going on," Boone said. "Pre-nuptial agreements are now de rigueur, I understand."

She hated those, was Jane's explosive reply. Besides, there was nothing new about them—here she referred him to any Victorian novel. "A friend of mine—a lawyer, naturally—drew one up for herself and her fiancé and showed it to me. I told her it looked to me like the contract my mother signed when she wanted her kitchen redone." She gave a little snort of laughter. "Which, in spite of all those escape clauses, she had a hard time getting out of when she changed her mind and decided to move upstate."

Marriage was not a subject Boone wished to linger on. He shifted his position so that they were no longer touching and made as if to go to sleep. Jane jerked at the sheet, asserting her right to full coverage, and demanded to know what he thought of hyperfiction.

At least she was changing the subject, Boone thought, even as he groaned and covered his head. "Don't!" he pleaded, "the very word makes me hyperventilate." A junior member of the faculty, burdened with freshman survey courses in English literature and remedial composition, he was fast losing interest in both literature and teaching, yet at the mere mention of computer novels with the kaleidoscopic fracturing and rearranging that made for hypertext, he felt all the rage of a Luddite foreseeing the obsolescence of his hand-loom.

Jane, who had a cozier relationship with her computer and, in fact, wasted a great deal of time playing computer games (she had become highly skilled at picking her way through land mines), giggled at his revulsion. It was the text, not the hypertext, she was talking about, she explained condescendingly. One in particular, about a New Age couple who achieved perfect union through tantric sex exercises—here, for a moment, Boone came awake—literally sharing life in each other's bodies. "Touching like this," Jane said, rubbing up against him, "wasn't enough for them, they had to be actually inside each other."

Boone made a retching sound, called on his Savior.

"Exactly," Jane said, "but that's not the point. The point is—"

The point to Boone was that she had no idea what tantric sex exercises were, as he now forced her to admit.

"The point is," Jane insisted, "that such a—such a pre-Gutenberg ideal of marriage, two becoming one—should still persist, I find incredible. I can't imagine anything more horrible. In fact, I have a recurrent nightmare about it. I'm in the kitchen, whipping up a soufflé—it's always a soufflé, which immediately sets a tone of disaster—worrying that he, my husband, will not be home in time, mea culpa, of course, I have started making it too early, when I hear the door open and there he is, though who he is I never see because it's like the camera is fixed on me, but I run into his arms, holding the dripping whisk, and he gives me a great bear hug and I'm deliriously happy to be so loved, so safe, although I'm a little awkward because I don't want to drip the gooey stuff on his jacket while he is kissing my neck, but then the kisses turn into nibbles, which really begin to hurt, and suddenly I realize those aren't nibbles, those are real bites, there are these gaping holes in my neck, he's actually eating me—and that's when I wake up. Wouldn't you call that a significant dream?"

Boone's reply was slow heavy breathing. He hated hearing other people's dreams. And if he answered, it would only be to disagree. Two becoming one sounded to him ideal—an ideal, by definition, being something that never materialized. A realist such as he accepted marriage as an inevitable stage of life, somewhere between puberty and old age, preferably coinciding with the first signs of balding. Comfortably aware of his still thick brush of hair—why do you cut it so short, every barber complained, you've nothing to hide—he saw no present need to think about it. Instead, as always when confronted with conjectures about the future, he thought pityingly of his sister. Poor Irene.

He was really asleep, Jane finally realized in the middle of recounting another dream she had just remembered, even more interesting. Disgruntled, she followed suit, consoling herself with the thought that at least she had nothing to fear from him in the way of a consuming passion.

One year and two months later, they were married.

Chapter 1

Now they had left behind the pretty country, the up and down terrain of amateurish delights. This was flat professional land, a rectilinear monotony of grain. Greenness as obsession. Midsummer madness.

"Fertility can be carried to excess," Jane Mayhew Everready said and another long honeymoon silence was broken.

"We can have two and still keep zero population growth." A self-appreciative laugh, short, sharp, as precisely on cue as a hired claque's. One hand kept rein on the wheel, the other squeezed her knee painfully.

"Oh Boone," she said, a two-year lovership culminating in this moment of maidenly disgust. "I meant all that grass out there. Wheat? Oats? Barley? What?"

He shrugged his ignorance, and she felt fully justified in having displaced the hand, aborting the expedition of fingers up her thigh. Not to even know the name. They were going to be farmers, he had assured her, an assurance as brash as the wedding ring which glinted in the sunlight, bigger, fatter, seemingly more golden than hers. And at the moment as much a fake as the one he used to wear.

If you want to come with me, we'll have to get married. Where he was going was real country, beyond all suburbs, to which the new morality could not be transported. Such was his proposal, as for a journey mapped on yellow parchment (note the four corners of the earth guarded by dragons and all the weight of the universe supported on the back of one small turtle.)

There was no denying that, for Boone, the inheritance had been remarkably opportune, the lawyer's letter arriving on the day his department chairman, pleading budget restraints, had advised him there were no more tenure tracks. A disgruntlement Boone had generously invited her to share: her fluency in romance languages was wasted on commercial documents and business letters; supported by their farm, she could venture into the free-lance field, translate works of more literary appeal.

Hers had been a talmudic acceptance: why not? She was as sick of the city as he. And if living together had failed them before, living apart had proved no better. He had moved into her apartment, and two months later they had split. She had moved into his apartment, and that had not lasted out the year. In each case, one had invaded the other's turf, no wonder the relationship failed. There must be something there, or so Jane reasoned out her yes, since they kept coming back together, like prodigals who had spent themselves on strangers, grateful now for even this parsimony of affection. So why not a fresh start, leaving their pasts as emigrants once left the old country to adventure to America, to a new world unowned by either.

Correction. Owned by Boone, once the will passed through probate. But owned in absentia until now, never invested with his presence, his belongings, his habits, his history. Land as virgin and unplowed to him as to her, descending to him from an Uncle Eban and Aunt Flo he had seen but once on a childhood visit. A great-aunt, great-uncle.

"Married sixty-seven years. She was eighty-four when she died. He couldn't stand it without her. Hung himself in the barn."

Now that was a marriage. Uncle Eban dangling from a rafter swung slowly before her eyes as she marched down the aisle on her father's arm. *With this ring I thee wed.* A promise to hang himself once she was dead.

"At least I know that's corn," Boone was pleased to announce. Still young corn, little more than waist-high. Baby ears, tightly sheathed in green, hardly visible at the base of the long leaves. To the right, to the left, as far ahead as the flat distance carried, the green marched across the land, a rally of totalitarian force.

To come upon a little handkerchief square of hard-packed dirt was perversely refreshing. An oasis in reverse, on which nothing grew but a general store. Grey weathered boards and a tin roof that extended beyond the frame to make a flimsy porch. In its shade, the coke machine looked as derelict and obsolete as war materiel after an army's retreat, but it was cold to the touch. With a parched cry of incredulous joy, Jane demanded change, fed the coins into the slot, received a sweating can from the rusty gullet.

"Me too," Boone said, now that he saw the machine worked, and tossed her more coins before entering the store.

A bell tinkled with the opening of the screen door. Boone waited in the dusky barn-like interior for someone to respond. Groceries on the left. Hardware, work clothes and shotguns on the right. From wire strung overhead bobbed plastic jugs and picnic ware, brightly colored as Japanese lanterns. Boone rapped on the grocery counter, and filled the time of waiting with an inventory of the shelves: cans, jars, cereal boxes—everything jumbo-size. The cash register was a work of art, with curlicues of brass over a dull silvery base, and archaic typewriter keys. From a top shelf, the small quivering face of a mouse appeared. He saw in the base of a cereal box a neatly gnawed hole.

From the silence, he might be waiting for a man dead twenty, forty years. But the bread on the counter was fresh. Huge sandwich loaves with familiar wholesome wonderful tasty names, pillow-soft to the touch. Reassured, Boone opened and shut the screen door again, to make the bell tinkle. What sort of a man would tend this patch of mercantile barrenness? Through the screen, Boone looked out beyond the tiny dirt yard to the enormity of green. A cereal box out there—jumbo size. And this foraging mouse of a storekeeper had scampered off. But was he a mouse, the man who kept this store, (where would I go if I left here?)? Or was he a hero, one who had challenged that monolithic power outside and held his ground—bare ground?

The word game. The good-word/bad-word game. A grin of reminiscence lit up Boone's thoughts. Long car trips of childhood and his father at the wheel. The word game, instructional while amusing, like those educational toys made of varnished unpainted wood, instead of the bright plastic kinetic robots or spaceships or laser guns Boone and his sister preferred . . .

Aware of the rear-view mirror, Irene watched the scenery from her side window and kicked her brother hard on the shins. Three years younger, two inches shorter, ten pounds lighter, Boone retorted by punching her in the ribs.

"I saw that, Boone." The father eye in the rear view mirror. All-knowing Masonic symbol, the eye in the effulgent triangle above the pyramid on the back of the one-dollar bill. God's stern eye, always fixed on him.

His mother, on the other hand, had to twist her head around, a movement which sent her head bobbing up and down, up and down, like those stupid toy dogs perched on the back seat of cars. "Why do you start these things, Boone? And then come crying to us when she beats you up?"

"A fighter. Boone's a fighter." Divine wrath replaced by peda-gogical fervor. "Now there's a good word for that, I'm sure. High-spirited. That's not bad. High-spirited is the good word, Irene. And what is a bad word for this particular attribute of Boone's?"

"Stupid."

"No, no. Belligerent. Better yet, bellicose. Quarrelsome."

Irene had a point though, his mother remarked. Boone should learn to pick a fight with someone his own size.

"Well, there's a good word for that too. Courageous, I call Boone. And you, Irene, you might call him—?"

"Stupid."

Father's calm instructional voice began to ravel at the edges. He reminded her of the rules of the game.

"Rash. Foolhardy. Reckless. Pay attention, girl, I'm trying to broaden your vocabulary." Stubborn, he suggested was a word that described her, but even that discommodious trait could be placed in a more favorable light. "Not stubborn, but—? All right, Boone, but what?"

"Stupid."

Stubborn, mule-headed/persevering, determined Irene: "Now that he's had half my candy, he says he's changed his mind, he won't buy any with his money at our next stop|"

Thrifty/stingy was the choice father offered her, but stupid, stupid, stupid was the word their lips formed, their breath wafted back and forth, silent and airy as the feathered bird in a badminton game, until Boone mouthed mother-fucker and father, eye in the mirror, pulled up on the side of the road . . .

From behind the stiff new denim of a hanging pair of overalls, an old man appeared and shuffled his way to the counter. Somewhere back there must be a cot, for his clothes were permeated with the drugged sleep of hot afternoon and his thin hair stood out in sweat-sodden clumps, as if his dream had tweaked and teased. A face, whose strength ran all to nose, leaving the eyes weak, the mouth mean.

Boone paid for a pack of cigarettes, and in spite of the fact that the register sent up a little flag marked "No Sale," deemed himself officially a customer, entitled now to ask for directions.

"Eban Sopher's farm? If you come through Rowena, you come the long way." Behind glasses, the watery eyes swam, pale blue globular fish still netted in the red veins of sleep. Finding Boone in error brought him fully awake, made his day. In the dust on the counter, he drew long straight lines intersected by other long straight lines, pointing out how Boone should have come.

"Yes, yes, I see, but now that I'm here, how do I get there?"

At this interest more than academic, the old man gaped. "You ain't one of *them*, are you? You don't dress their way. Who you looking for out there?"

Boone expressed his irritation by squeezing in and out the nearest pneumatic loaf of bread and identified himself as Eban Sopher's nephew. Great-nephew.

"Ha. Eban Sopher's dead." Once again a twitch of triumph, a self-congratulatory smirk at knowing more than this stranger did. "Hung himself six, seven months ago. Last fall, it was."

Testily Boone said that he knew. He was Eban Sopher's heir. The farm was now his. If he could ever find it, that is.

Was he kicking them out then, the whole lot and caboodle? And did they know?

If he meant Mr. Windigo, Boone admitted the man's lease of the property had another three months to go. Mr. Windigo was fully aware of Boone's plan not to renew the lease but to operate the farm himself. Had been kind enough to invite him out as guest, so to speak, much as his great-uncle seemed to have been these few years. The whole lot and caboodle, though? A large family? Large families still the going thing around here, Boone supposed, looking up at the jumbo-sized cereal boxes. The growing thing, he almost said, still impressed by all the corn.

"Kids? No, they don't take in folks with kids." Windigo now. That would be the boss man, the leader of the flock.

Boone's heart sank. Oh God, not a commune. Were those still around? Besides, he had thought they were all in Vermont or California, huddled on the coasts like embryonic colonies in a brave new world.

"Nice enough folks. No drugs, no smoking, no drinking, no running around with their clothes off. People around here are pretty broadminded. Don't mind these new sects, so long as they're Christian and pay their taxes and don't mess around trying to convert other folks."

Boone's heart sank deeper, hearing such praise on this man's desiccated lips. Jesus freaks, no less. Well, flock or no, only a Mr. Windigo had signed the lease, and he had promptly acknowledged Boone's legal rights in recent correspondence. No mention of his religion, either as a plea or threat. Instead he had generously offered to teach the new owner some fundamentals of farming, should Boone care to come out ahead of time. Still Boone did not like this new role in which he was cast—the landlord evicting the good shepherd and his disciples—a natural, it sounded like, for a Cecil B. DeMille film. And he not Charlie Heston but the one who winds up under the chariot's wheels.

The directions, when he finally received them, were simple enough. No forks in the road, no diagonal shortcuts, no ambiguous curves. A mere matter of counting off the straight-lined squares on a checkerboard. A chess knight's move, two squares down and one square over, the squares delineated by roads reckoning off the land not in acres but in mile-square sections.

Out by the coke machine he collected Jane. She had guzzled down most of his can as well as her own. Most but not all. There was an alcoholic's cunning in leaving a few swigs, like a cleaning woman exercising restraint with the master's Scotch. He dug in his pockets, came up short. The cigarettes had taken his last loose change. Damn it, he swore, he was not about to tinkle that old man out of bed again.

My wife, he wondered: good word or bad?

Jane found the idea of a commune amusing. Giggles rose sporadically in her throat like the carbonated aftermath of all that coke, although Boone made it clear it took a coarser sensibility than his to find it funny. He had never relished the prospect of evicting even Mr. Windigo; now he found himself turning out a whole—he groped for the proper term of venery—flock, school, pride, herd?

Whole lot of people, he weakly settled for, just how many the storekeeper himself didn't know. Whole lot of people suited Jane just fine. She had not been aware of her depression, much as she was never aware of how listless, how drained of energy she was during a long heat wave until the spanking fresh cool air swept in, although in fact she had been steadily losing weight. Seven pounds in the seven days before the ceremony so that at the last minute deeper darts had to be basted in her wedding dress, for which she had to call on her super's wife again. But now with its lifting, she felt the true weight of that incubus, knew the exact moment it had settled itself on her. The wedding. No, before that, the moment a wedding had been decided upon. Since that moment she had dragged herself along like a fat woman on bunion-bulging feet, although in fact she had been steadily losing weight. Seven pounds in the seven days before the ceremony so that at the last minute deeper darts had to be basted in her wedding dress, for which she had to call on her super's wife.

Standing in her slip while the needle ran in and out of the heavy Italian silk, she watched Mrs. Caligor bite off the ends of the thread with a ravenous fierceness, wondered why so fat a woman would choose a cane-seated chair. "Don't ever lose that tiny waist, honey," Mrs. Caligor said, with a sigh that seemed to evaginate her soul. So a man turns inside out his pockets to show he has nothing left. So this loss of a tiny waist, seen now as her own fatal mistake, was proffered as the total sum of wisdom gained in a hard life.

Nor had her father the night before the wedding been of much help, although his mere presence, jetted up from a Florida golf course, was accepted by her in the spirit in which it was offered: as a rather magnificent wedding gift. He had opened the door of the hotel room, freshly shaved and shirted and tied, but still in boxer shorts. Boone dressed from the bottom up, her father from the top down—a difference she noted as highly significant. Let it never be said she had chosen a man just like the man who married dear old Mom.

His tan was the temperate well-maintained glow of one who did not have to cram in the sun and when she squeezed him, returning hug for hug, his body had the hard unripened feel of out-of-season fruit. "Come on, come on," he said, chucking her under the chin, "it's not the end of the world. Just remember, if it turns out to be a mistake, you can always cut your losses and run."

She supposed that was how he kept in such good shape—running. From one mistake to another. And only that first one, the marriage to her mother, had been costly. A beginner's gaucherie, before he had become practiced in the art of amicable divorce. From the bedroom, the hiss of hatred rising like steam heat in cold winter nights (don't wake the child|). Yet the sunny times, the reconciliations, were even worse, not taking the child into account at all. The battles had been bearable, held within the confines of classic drama, all blood and gore off-stage, made almost seemly by the regal stiffness of the actors, the measured speech before their audience of one. But hide from me your joy! the child's heart cried out, that Medusa head of sex rampant and satisfied that you shine full-face on me, the all-exclusive joy that turns me to stone!

"I've made my mistakes," she reproved her father, reminding him that the customs of her country were different and that his times were bygone. "If I marry Boone, it's because I know this is right."

I know, she had said. But even on the wedding eve, an iffiness still there.

If this isn't love, it will have to do, until the real thing comes along . . .her father sang in a smooth baritone as dated as the smooth melody. "A song of my youth. Has nostalgia reached back that far? Once, just once, I'd like that sung at a wedding. Your mother, as I recall, chose O Promise Me."

Her hand resting on his arm, they advanced down the aisle, the first and last example he gave of parental guidance. Beneath the processional Lohengrin, his subversive hum: until the real thing comes along . . .

Windigo. Boone would have sped by without seeing the grey splintery wood sign had she not screeched. He backed up, turned sharply into the narrow black-top lane. Sopher, the sign should read, he said. It was still Sopher land.

"It looks like Windigo's been there forever," she said. More corn, on both sides of them, as if they were traveling in a furrow. And then the path curved. A curve after all those straight lines. And the land rose. Very slightly, but Jane felt the undulation of the earth like a sexual stimulation. Through the window the late-afternoon slant of the sun baked her bare thighs. On their outside, the trickle of heat; inside the moisture of desire.

"Stop the car," she pleaded, as if something were suddenly wrong.

"For that?" Boone unlocked her arms, broke from her kiss as from the importunity of an unreasoning child. "Here? Now?"

Of course. The where and the when had to be of his choosing. The next time he made a grab for her, Jane sullenly vowed, she would not be there.

"We must be at least three inches above sea level now. Maybe we should name the house Hilltop Hall. Or how about Mountain View? Eagle's Roost?" She was lashing out at the land itself, as if it had betrayed her by promising to reach some great height, only to peter out in the same old flatness.

"You won't find a real hill this side of the river," Boone said. "The Sopher house is on top of an Indian burial mound, that accounts for the slight rise. Uncle Eban told me he plowed up Indian bones now and then when he first farmed here."

"What house?"

Before them a ten-foot-tall wire fence, its gate straddling the road. Heavy-gauge wire, bent inward at the top, constructed as to support some Danger! High Voltage! sign. Beyond it they could see long low sheds. A high hayloft barn. Two silos, one new and aluminum-bright, the other like an old wooden barrel whose staves had burst. But no house.

Boone sat frozen at the wheel as if he had stopped the car just before it went over a cliff. Shaken as if the front wheels still turned in mid-air. "I don't get it. It used to be there. *There.*" Slowly the car inched forward—Boone still testing the firmness of the ground underfoot. "Where that—that—what the hell is it, a circus tent?"

"A dome. A geodesic dome." Jane began to laugh, as much at Boone's discomfiture as at the unexpected structure which turned the dull rural scene into a child's puzzle picture: find the object which does not belong here. "Buck Fuller rides again," she giggled, "here of all places."

Boone's eyes still strained for the sight of a house he knew was there, which she, with clearer vision, could see was not. Slowly he drove through the half-open gate, passage just wide enough for the car, babbling on about the house. Wedded to the past. "It had three stories, a huge place, Victorian, I suppose. And a little tower on top. The crow's nest, Uncle Eban called it, and that's about how big it was. A platform at the top of the stairs and the one little window, round as a porthole. God, I remember that so clearly. I was no more than nine or ten that summer, but that I remember. Kneeling there, looking out the window . . .you know the kind of memory? Every damn detail of the scenery, but no people, no action, no meaning. Like a stage set at the moment the curtain rises, with the actors still in the wings . . . That was some house, I tell you."

Fifteen, twenty rooms, it sounded like. Angry at the mere thought of cleaning such a Victorian wife-killer, Jane announced her approval of the dome. Its peculiar piebald look was due to its unfinished state, she pointed out. Most of the triangular facets had a transparent plastic skin, reflecting at the moment a sunset red as blood, but a few had been covered with an opaque parchment-like material in varying warm earth tones. Obviously the plastic was a temporary expedient; in time the whole hemisphere would have an organic integument of striking patchwork design.

What had looked like acres of green lawn from a distance resolved into coarse pasture close at hand, scarred with the corrugated ruts made by heavy farm machinery. In the jouncing car, they could judge how dry the weather must have been.

"Where is everybody? Or anybody." The promise of a whole lot of people waited to be fulfilled. Those herringbone tracks seemed now like the spoor of dinosaurs preserved in petrified earth from a time when all had been primeval mud.

"Probably at supper. Early to bed, early to rise, the original daylight saving time." But the problem, as Boone saw it, was to locate the diners, since nothing looked like a house. The dome? It stood on the site of Uncle Eban's old house, he was sure, but he agreed with Jane that it had an unfinished look. Any light within would have shown through panels clear as glass, yet the belly-curve facing east, having lost the sun, looked as cold and lifeless as the dark side of the moon.

Bisected by the horizon, the sun was another geodesic dome, brightly bloodily alight. Jane shivered. It was as if they had landed in some spacecraft on a strange planet, whose breath was hot and fetid with life, but life in alien incommunicable form. Outside the circumference of the fence, the corn crackled as it grew, greenness growling, held in bay by tenuous wire. She and Boone alone. Man without mankind. Soon they would grunt instead of speak, like the last of a crazed crew stranded too long on a deserted isle.

In full panic, Jane reached over and slapped repeatedly on the horn as Boone cruised slowly on. A trio of Quonset huts now came into view, until now eclipsed by the dome. And people. Thank God, people. Breaking the bottleneck of narrow doorways, spewing out on the grass, advancing toward the car in eager response to those panic blasts. Lots of people, neatly divided into male and female by a uniform of sex: high-bibbed overalls for men, high-necked ankle-length calico gowns for the women. She threw a quick look at Boone, whose aversion to uniforms was stronger even than hers. Jesus, he groaned. No, she reassured him, just His R.O.T.C.

All of an age, Jane had the impression, as they drew closer—her and Boone's age. And in the forefront a loose-limbed giant (beneath the high bibs, all the male torsos were bare), with blond hair so thick its short straight cut looked beveled at the edge, a face stamped out of handsomeness. He is hurrying to *me*, Jane thought, to me. Hurrying with deliberate speed, keeping to the committee pace of welcome, not breaking rank, yet his heart bounding toward her. As hers sprang out of her keeping to meet him, all the while she sat wifely in the car by Boone's side. The motor stilled, it was another hum she heard . . . *the real thing*. The real thing had come along.

There was something tentative about the way Boone got out of the car. To ask for clearer directions, it would seem, or merely to stretch cramped legs, or use the john—as if he were not aware they had come to their final stop. And there was a matching hesitancy in the advance of the group, a wavering halt just beyond the bounds of welcome. The wall of denim parted, the kaleidoscope of calico print rearranged itself. In the forefront emerged one of shorter stature, slower stride. Behind him a stilled tableau proclaimed: this is the leader.

"Everready?"

Boone nodded, held out his hand. "Mr. Windigo?"

Jane let out a hoot of nervous laughter. Historic encounter in the jungle. And she had thought the jungle was what they were leaving behind. "Wish I were going with you," Boone's father had said at the moment of farewell, looking strangely shabby, as if his recent widowhood had left him stripped of decent outer garments. "This city has become a jungle."

"The new owners," said the leader of the flock in the voice of one bestowing a benediction. "The Society of Elath has been expecting you. Good evening. And welcome."

From within the dome came a deep lugubrious sound, as from some primitive woodwind long as an alpenhorn. An instrument built to mimic the grumble of the earth before a quake, the groan of mountains before an avalanche.

"The Feast of Elath," Mr. Windigo said with a Jovian nod. "It begins."

Chapter II

The Windigo, he was called. As in The MacGregor, The Stuart, The MacTavish. Chieftain of a clan. A fitting mode of address for a man whose aura of authority all but crackled in the air. ("How old do you think he is? I don't like it when you can't tell," was Jane's first private comment. "And have you ever seen such a big ugly head?")

Yet Boone admired the monumental head. The thick and curly hair was cropped so close it seemed a spongy growth, iron-grey moss on iron-grey stone, softening but not obscuring the massive sculpture of the skull. A primitive sculpture, broad and flattened. An Olmec head, squashed boxer's nose, greyish skin pitted like granite, and full-lipped mouth that sneered at the senses and settled for power. All the more striking in that harsh setting were the large brown liquid eyes, Hindu eyes of a divine bovinity.

Orders were given, coated in kindness, phrased as suggestion, but orders nonetheless. "Good evening," he had commanded the heavens, and now he decreed that the new arrivals were tired, they would want to settle in, get a good night's sleep, save the introduction to their new home until the morning. Rafe would show them to their quarters, temporary but The Windigo hoped sufficiently comfortable. Melissa would bring them a bite to eat since they had arrived too late for supper.

"Too late?" Boone caught Jane's aghast whisper. "My God, the sun is just setting."

"And they'll be up when it rises—I warned you, didn't I?" Boone whispered back, knowing no pity for a woman who grandly proclaimed "I'm a night person," and weekends stayed in bed until noon, and then in bare feet and limp nylon nightie made a leisurely brunch (hideous word, hideous elision of meals, euphemism for sleeping half one's life away). *We're eating into our principal* was his father's panic as his mother wasted away in and out of hospitals. Time was Boone's principal, on which he drew interest only when awake, and oh, the limited capital of his days. Already he approved of this new rhythm of life, could foresee the healthy leap out of bed at daybreak, the decontaminating scrub-down in a cold shower, the hearty farmer's breakfast of country-cured ham and home fries, then out the door to blink at sunlight still on the early-morning horizontal, the whole day before him like a bright juicy apple with not a single bite taken.

"This is the way man was meant to live, Jane," he said, feeling the assurance of one who has opened fresh instructions from God. "You'll like it, you'll see."

She gave him a non-believer's snort and attacked on the bias. "Are you going to let him carry *all* the bags?"

The tall blond man waited patiently, two bags in hand, two clutched under arm. He was the one whom Boone had thought the leader until The Windigo appeared. "No sweat," he said, rejecting Boone's offer, and led the way toward the distant barn. "I could have sworn the barn was in the other direction," Boone muttered, marveling at the displacements of memory.

"You're always turned around," Jane muttered back. "We'd never get any place if I didn't tell you which way to go." Just as he decided they should have taken the car, he heard the motor start. Another order had been given. The car was being driven away.

They entered high-raftered darkness. The flick of a wall switch lit a naked bulb dangling over rickety-looking stairs, steeply pitched, little more than a ladder permanently affixed. He knew immediately this was not the cow barn he remembered. This was a horse barn, long empty of horses, not even the smells remembered. A place for junk, for discards that would not burn easily, for worn rubber and rusted metal parts of machines whose very purpose was no longer known. Even a museum piece or two, like the two-wheeled buggy with rotted folding top, pitched forward on its shafts, a submissive genuflection to passing times. Yet it was here that Uncle Eban had spent his last years.

"After his house burned down," their guide explained.

So that was what had happened to the house. Burned down. Boone felt vindicated, as if even its prior existence had been under question. When did it happen, he asked, and hadn't it stood where the dome was now? Right again, he congratulated his memory. And right again—he gave Jane a triumphant look—the cow barn close by had burned down too.

As to when, that was before Rafe's time. "Soon after The Windigo arrived, I think. That was when the old man fixed the loft upstairs into an apartment. We use it for guests now, it gives them a certain privacy. Not everyone takes immediately to our dormitory-style of living. Watch the stairs, they're steep as hell, and a little shaky underfoot."

Just as advertised, Rafe made it up with no sweat—a feat which left Boone morosely aware of his own sticky shirt. Carrying nothing, he had yet found it hard to keep up with Rafe's brisk pace. No more smoking, he resolved, and crushed the wilted cigarette package in his pocket, remembering at the same moment, with relief, that an unopened carton lay in one of those bags.

"What's keeping you?" he called down to Jane.

She was staring up at the rafters, one foot still on the bottom step, and he thought immediately of bats. Too many vampire movies as a kid, he knew, but still the skin on the back of his neck crawled. The ears, he always saw them going for the ears. Not there, he would snap, even when Jane tongued him with passion. Not in the porches of my ear.

"Do you see anything?" he asked anxiously.

Her 'no' was drawn out with disappointment.

"Wedding is destiny, hanging likewise."

Intoned, not spoken, the words came at him from behind. Boone saw a startled look on Jane's upturned face and remembered what besides old tubing, rusty chains and a worn horse collar must have hung there once. This stranger was more privy to his wife's thoughts than he.

"An old saw?" There was a cuckold's bitterness in the sneer.

"Dunno. Sounds like one. First time I heard it was at your uncle's funeral. The Windigo gave the eulogy, since there was no family here. Beautiful service, man, beautiful."

Behind a raw wood door lay their quarters. Boone sank into the depression of a lumpy daybed, keeping company with his shame at having had no thought of Uncle Eban either pendulous or erect. Jane, giddy as a bride just hoisted over the threshold, showed off a housewifely competence by pulling out drawers, locating the bathroom, and breathlessly remarking that she did not know how they were expected to manage with only a small sink and a hot plate for a kitchen.

"Rafe—that is your name, isn't it?" she asked. "How long have you been a member of this commune?" All that breathlessness had been but a hurrying to this point, as in those long overdue letters home scrawled in haste to reach the p.s.: please send money. What she really wanted to know, Boone interpreted, was what a gorgeous guy like that was doing in a place like this.

The gorgeous guy was not exactly pleased. His small smile was more of a grimace. "Hey, hey, hey. Don't use that word, commune. Everyone makes the same mistake, it's a drag. That hippie kind of scene, people coming and going and the whole works folding in a year or two— that's all history. We're different. We are here to stay."

Boone sat up sharply. Until I kick you out, he thought angrily. As soon as the damn lease is up.

"Not to stay *here*," Jane interpreted quickly. "Here to *stay*."

"So what do you call this—" Boone placed tongue in cheek and let go—"this cohesive effort at a productive way of life devoted to re-establishing old verities no longer found in the polluted mainstream of modern industrial civilization?"

Rafe favored him with a suspicious look. "Was that the first time you met The Windigo, back there?"

Boone crossed his heart, cherishing the accuracy of his aim. "The very first time." And saluted his father: good word/bad word was still the game. Not commune, society. The Society of Elath. Clever man, this Windigo. The word commune sounded too much like communism, evoking visions of anarchy, godlessness, drugs, sex, nudity, and other unsanitary conditions imperiling the town's water supply. But society, now there was a word with good vibes. Not rebels against, but adherents of. High society. Society of Jesus. Society as a Whole. The Establishment itself.

Rafe resumed the role of bellhop pointing out the amenities. "The tub is an old one your uncle picked up somewhere. Funny how small people must have been back then. I have to warn you about that hot plate, it'll take an hour to boil a pot of water, if it works at all. The Windigo suggests you take your meals with us."

Another order. It was only temporary, Boone found it necessary to remember. The raw timbered walls, on which spider webs gleamed like hoarfrost, the splintery floor, the furnishings all "picked up somewhere," most likely the town dump. The bed he was sitting on, Rafe demonstrated, was the hi-riser kind, from beneath which another bed could be drawn, raised, and used as a twin, separate or Siamese. A slight hesitation. Or did Boone merely imagine a flicker of puritanical distaste before he was shown how the beds could be joined? This Golden Boy with the bare folk-hero chest.

Boone's spirits momentarily lifted, but were still no match for Jane's. Those last wearing hours of the trip she had sulked, snapped, been at times downright unpleasant. Now, with a legitimate grievance to voice (this was the rural Eden to which she had been brought?) she was ringing out the changes of delight with a trained musical laugh (that pre-Raphaelite arch of throat had been achieved by much practice before a mirror, she had once confessed). If Rafe had cracked a joke, Boone had missed it. She was a brown girl, of a brownness that turned sallow in discontent, but looking at her now, Boone thought of glowing topaz, polished amber, light-streaked shining cats-eye. My semi-precious Jane. Listening so intently, her whole body in receptive pose, and to what? A dietary diatribe.

"No meat at all? Is it because of —you know, ethical scruples? Or just because you think it's healthier?"

"Because that's all the human body needs. Whole grains, fruit, goat's milk and cheese. After a week or two, you'll find you never felt better in your life."

Inwardly Boone groaned. The only thing more boring than a religious freak was a health nut, and here they had stumbled on both. The Hunta diet, Rafe earnestly explained. All Huntas lived to be 126 with every tooth in their mouth. Boone could believe the teeth. Rafe's were white and even, looking as improbably perfect as those zoomed in on for a toothpaste commercial.

"This supper," Boone ventured, "I hope we're not putting you folks out."

"Sorry," Rafe said, "I know how hungry you two must be. Melissa will be here any minute."

"Poor Boone," Jane apologized, "he has to have his three square meals a day." Baby has to have his two a.m. bottle, the apology implied. Boone kindled the small brushfire of anger with fresh remembrance from the trip's log. She had been apologizing for him from the moment she had been officially dubbed his wife. To the garage mechanic in Pittsfield, when Boone protested that a front-wheel realignment did not address the problem, a peculiar noise he heard in the rear. "My husband, I'm afraid, hears things as soon as he gets in that car of his." But no apology to him when the bearings in the right rear wheel burnt out and the axle, crystallized by heat, had cracked in two . . . To the motel manager outside Daytona, who claimed to have received no reservation request. Incompetent ass and more, Boone had called him. "My husband, I'm afraid, is sometimes absent-minded. The typical professor, you know." Assistant professor, Boone had corrected her loudly, not even that anymore. Fired, he had yelled over his shoulder as Jane pulled him away, for sexual harassment! In the crummy cabin they found further down the highway, she wept because he had embarrassed her. He was now in the same category as a broken bra strap or a menstrual bloodstain that had seeped through.

The creaking of the barn door meant that succor had come. At the sound, Jane cocked her head, betrayed herself with one quick hungry look.

"Melissa," Rafe confirmed.

Boone's grunt of satisfaction had to stand alone. Jane made a point of not being interested, not at all. She was fully occupied with rummaging through the one empty closet. Nothing therein but bent wire hangers, rattling skeletons of dead clothes.

"Hey, look what somebody left in here. I wonder who." A puddle of jersey lay on the floor. She picked it up and gave a soft "wow" at its sexy cut. The way she held the dress against her body, jutting her hips forward, was clearly a question. It was not so clear from whom she wanted an answer.

"Yeah, nice," Boone said.

Rafe's frown signified not so much disapproval as laboring thought. "It belonged to my wife, I think. We stayed here ourselves when we first arrived."

Abruptly Jane held the dress out at arm's length. My wife, the man just said, and behold Creusa seared by the poison of Medea's golden robe. For a moment his anger detoured to his sourly laboring, dully resentful students, who found nothing of use in the works of dead white males. Ex-students. (No, he was the ex.) For them, the movies said it all. For them, an ancient legend was James Dean.

"If you like it, it's yours," Rafe said as supper crossed the threshold. "We have no use for such clothes here."

The woman who entered was as blond, as tall as Rafe, with features of undistinguished evenness. The hair was her beauty, twisted into two long ropes, each as thick as a hawser. So this was Melissa. For the moment, Boone's interest was more focused on the tray. So that was supper. A large fruit tart. And a pitcher of milk. That was it? That was all?

"The apricots are fresh, not canned," Melissa informed him. So she misread the concern in his eyes. "And the milk from our own goats." Warm from the nanny's tits. More nourishing, more easily digestible than cow's, but they might have to get used to the taste. To the fact that milk had any taste at all. And having briskly arranged two settings and partitioned the tart, Melissa moved back and took up her station beside Rafe.

The advertised privacy was yet to materialize. "Please," he and Jane were urged. "Won't you—?" Jane asked, but no, they were to eat alone, under the benign gaze of these two fine specimens of the perfect diet. A little like screwing in Macy's window, this eating while others watched. The table was long and narrow, never meant for dining. In the front hall of some old country house it had once urbanely received gentlemen's hats and ladies' gloves, calling Boone chewed cards and brown-wrapped parcels from the post. They were perforce seated side by side, not across. Like feeding at a trough. carefully. Mouth closed. No noise. Mastication in public. An obscenity to be deplored.

The tart was good, Jane said more than once. Good, Boone announced to the audience. Melissa's smile spread slowly, like film in its developing bath. The cutting edge of hunger dulled, Boone could eye her more dispassionately. Statuesque blonde. Boone rose from the table, satisfied. The archaic phrase was right. She was pre-suffrage, something about her bringing to mind lofty pompadours, tiny waists, the fine pen strokes of Charles Dana Gibson. Those mutton-sleeved beauties. Forget their Mussolini chins, think only of their willowy grace, their starched poise. Never were women's bodies more erotic than under all those clothes, moving with the languor of the big cats in a circus act, whipsnapped into balancing on pedestals. (Forget those managerial faces.) Yes, indeedy, women knew then how to stand still and be looked at. As Melissa stood now, while he looked at her. As Rafe stood, Boone noticed with a flicker of attention, while Jane looked at him.

"You haven't touched your milk," Melissa said gently.

Not as bad as he had feared. Not bad at all. Unexpectedly tangy. But it was the warmth that got to him, sending off shock waves of near-recognition. Breast-warm sticky trickle out of the corner of his mouth. Melissa was gravely awaiting his judgment. He felt a deep shame as if caught in the acting out of a perverted fantasy.

"Great stuff," he proclaimed.

"Good, this still ticks," Rafe said, winding an old alarm clock. "You may need it the first few days. Breakfast's at six."

"Six?" Love's ardor had cooled. There was no music in Jane's screech.

Melissa had gathered their dishes, reloaded the tray. For this purpose (in prison no cutlery is left behind), they had stayed? "You will be surprised how quickly your body relearns its natural rhythms, and you won't need that ugly sound. Who wants to awaken to alarm? Sunrise and sunset are the high and low tides of our blood's flow."

"I'm sure," Jane agreed politely. "But it seems to me—" She turned to Boone with her desperate proposition. "It occurs to me, Boone, we have no right to impose. The first thing in the morning, we'll drive into town, pick up one of those tabletop broiler ovens, a few pots and pans, and fix up some kind of a working kitchen here. Then we won't get in anybody's way."

In other words, let them have the sunrise to sunset shift, she would stick to noon and midnight. But there was merit to her thought. Keeping their own hours, eating their own kind of food, they would be a little more than guest, though still a little less than owners of this land.

"I'm sorry, but didn't Rafe explain?" Melissa asked.

Rafe was sorry too, but he thought they understood. Had not The Windigo himself announced that the Feast of Elath had begun?

"What's that to do with us?"

"The horn has blown," Melissa said, explaining all.

"The gates are closed," Rafe said. "They won't be opened until Elath is over and the horn is blown again."

"You're saying we can't go out? That's impossible! We brought just our clothes. We need things!" Jane's fists were clenched, a sign Boone knew well, alerted by the childhood stories they had told each other in their salad days of love. Stories of the child Boone. And the child Jane: *I was never spanked, they locked me in my room for punishment. And then made love in their bedroom directly underneath. The one time they needn't fear my suddenly opening their door and cutely prancing in. But not for long, I saw to that. I'd throw myself down on the floor and scream and pound away with my fists until their ceiling showed little cracks and plaster dust rubbed like gravel in their sheets.*

Boone spoke to soothe. She might scream yet, and pound the floor. She did not take well to being locked in. Or locked out.

"We can stick it out, Jane, it's only for a day or two."

"Seven," Rafe corrected. "It takes six days to prepare, on the seventh the Feast is served."

Jane readied herself to screech again, but "Please," Melissa urged, "I'm sure we can provide all you need."

There seemed no help for it. In the end, Jane surrendered. To Rafe, her eyes said, "I suppose we just happened to arrive at the wrong time."

"Oh, no"—protest breathed in unison by the two disciples of this strange sect. Grave courtesy held them for a moment on the threshold of departure, like paired caryatids employed on either side of an imposing temple door. Paired? Was this woman with the unvarnished face and long granny gown the same wife who had arrived in that slinky bit of brief high fashion? Boone saw his wonderment shared by Jane, but she had her own way of asking that question.

"Melissa, you're sure you no longer want this?"

There was no interest, no recognition in the shrug Melissa gave the chair back to which the soft jersey clung. "Such clothes belong to no one here." And Boone cackled at that answer, which told Jane nothing about who belonged to Rafe.

They were private now.

"Okay. Let's talk about it."

"Talk?" she shot back with military precision. "When has talk ever solved anything?"

"Fuck you," he replied. In grim silence he pulled out and up the hi-riser, linking together the two beds. She crawled in beside him, miming great fatigue with an extravagant yawn. He checked the alarm clock, which was missing a leg and reclined on its back, seemingly as exhausted as she, and then fuck her he did. With a vengeance. Big with vengeance. Rape, she implied, turning her head away from his kisses. But she climaxed all the same. He fucked her into a sweating liquid pulp and with her juices matting the hairs on his thigh, he heard her cry out.

"I hate you, hate you, hate you."

Almost instantly asleep, he mumbled back. "Love. Love you, Jane."

Chapter III

Boone counted heads at the communal breakfast. Seventeen, excluding Jane and himself. Last night the welcoming horde had seemed like more. The three tables were placed in conventional banquet style, two parallel, joined at one end by the third crosswise. There The Windigo sat, centered to divide the men on his right, the women on his left. An unexpected division. No separation of the sexes had been evident in the two dormitory huts, whose doors stood open. On their way over, he and Jane had noticed the early morning bustle: a random mix of overalled and calicoed figures bending over narrow hard-looking bunks, trimming the coarse grey blankets with precise hospital corners. Prurience was feared more at table than in bed, it would seem.

"Let us renew our Vow," The Windigo said, and heads were bowed. The vow, or whatever grace was sought, filled a moment of silence. Who was at the other end of the line, Boone wondered. Father? Son? Some clown named Elath? He had yet to hear Jesus' name, a strange continence for Jesus freaks. Freaks they undoubtedly were, but some other sobriquet was required. Stiff-necked and open-eyed, Boone surveyed the smoothly combed male crowns, the naked female center parts from which the hair was drawn so tightly he wondered it did not hurt. All the women wore braids, but only Melissa's—ah, that treacle of a name!—were so erotically thick, the hair swelling out of its constrictive plaiting like tumescent sex.

From his tail-end seat at the men's table, he looked across to Jane, seated in direct opposition, the last among the women. Their own vow, his winked to remind her, had been renewed last night in bed. But she sat slumped in her seat, head bowed along with the rest. Deliberately avoiding his eye? More likely asleep in her seat. This six a.m. breakfast was not her cup of tea and she looked it. The crust of sleep was still in her eyes, the wrinkled bed linen imprinted on her cheek, the dampness of night-sweat made tendrils of the loose front edges of her hair. Sleep stuck to her like a grubby child's sweat. Love, love you, Jane. But his message was not received. A difference in circadian rhythm. Different time zones. His Mondays still her Sundays.

The prayer was over, but there was an unremarked tag-end of ritual which Boone almost missed, so intent was he on catching all the farm shop talk, every disjointed murmur from which he might begin to learn his new trade. He had not felt so modestly aware of ignorance since freshman high-school days when he had loitered in the locker room, assiduously tying and retying his gym shoes, picking up the jock talk of sex.

An elbow dig from his neighbor, Rafe, alerted him to the little bowl of dried corn kernels which had been passed down the table. "Take one of each color," Rafe instructed.

Red. Black. Yellow. White. Hard to believe corn came in so many colors. He recalled the dried varicolored ears of "Indian" corn, sold by florists in the city around Halloween time. The harvest motif, hung on apartment doors that in a few weeks would bear Christmas wreaths. But were they really edible? Another little bowl, of the same unglazed reddish clay reminiscent of the common flower pot, was making its way down the women's side. He checked out Jane. Unhesitatingly she picked out four kernels, popped them into her mouth and, employing the etiquette for finger food, made a play with her napkin, dabbing her lips. He followed her lead, but omitted that meretricious refinement.

He found the toasted kernels salty, tough and chewy. But tasty. Possibly addictive, like cocktail peanuts or potato chips. Automatically his hand strayed to the bowl for a refill but, with a look of silent reproof (did one take seconds of communion wine and wafers?), Rafe sent the bowl back on its return journey to The Windigo.

The conversation was proving less informative than Boone had hoped. An amicable detailing of chores was all he could catch. The digging of a barbecue pit aroused mild contention. Clean the old one out, some said. No, dig it anew, the others disagreed.

Crunching on granola-type cereal, Boone recalled the vegetarian ardor with which they had been fed the night before. "Hey," he said to the blond hulk beside him, "I thought you said no meat. Whole grains, nuts, fruit, goat's milk, cheese—and live forever. What the hell is there in that list you can barbecue?"

Rafe explained with the patience due a novitiate. "It's the Feast of Elath, remember. There will be roast kid tonight." And every night of the Holy Week, Boone was graciously informed, until that presumably religious, certainly culinary, climax on the seventh—the Feast itself.

"Let me help with the digging," Boone offered, as the chairs were pushed back. For that he had sufficient expertise, he suggested in modest self-deprecation. Rafe slapped him on the back, an accolade of sorts.

"You're to go with The Windigo."

And Jane? Jane was encircled by the women. A dark-haired woman was whispering in her ear. Sharp-nosed, sharp-chinned, thin-lipped—the kind of face that in time would shrivel into the caricature of a witch. Jane was swept away, Melissa's arm snaked around her waist, Boone's eyes still on her. That was his white shirt she wore, the tails brought forward and knotted under the ribcage, leaving exposed a wide belt of nakedness above the tight jeans riding on her hips. Awash in that sea of calico, her shirted trousered figure, bulging fore and aft, looked epicene.

It was a coldly critical thought, impersonal in its vision, as shocking to Boone as the encounter of his own image in an unexpected mirror, when in that brief second before recognition restored him to his familiar self he made some half-formed, near-contemptuous judgment. But he had never caught Jane out that way. That's Jane, his eyes would tell him immediately, the name an entity, self-describing. His Jane. Existing in his consciousness, embedded in his being like a pearl in an oyster. I love her, therefore she is.

No, he never looked at Jane as if she were an alien life form just landed on his private planet. That was her kind of look, unpredictable and deadly as a guerilla attack: when she was waiting for him on some appointed street corner and he surprised her by coming up behind; when in bitter parody of that *South Pacific* tune they saw each other, through the haze of hash, across a crowded room; when on some Sunday he rejoined her in bed, turning sloth to good account, and they lay sweating, loose-jointed, intertwined, eyeball to eyeball, and in the opened shutter of her pupils, he would see his reduced image, her summing up of him. A critical evaluation. A term report. Attack, attack, attack—the von Clausewitz of the boudoir. Last night? Rape, rape! her stony silence had shrieked, hardening his excitement to an excruciating pitch. (God, what a fuck, she couldn't find fault with that!) Preemptive. Purely preemptive. The manly art of self-defense.

She had vanished with the women, but her parting smile—directed at Rafe, not him—still lingered in the room, Smiles could do that (vide the Cheshire cat). .

In the hut that served as kitchen, Jane watched the making of bread. The stove was a mammoth wood-burning affair, spit-and-polish black, looming against the wall like some well-tended baal.

"Would you like to try it?" Carla moved aside at the flour-dusted table. "Kneading is fun." From the heat or the muscular exertion, her sharp face had become as shiny as the dough. She was the boss, Jane decided with some amusement, in spite of the busy pretense of egalitarian anarchy. Vague and indirect as were her commands—shouldn't we? would anyone like to? hadn't someone better?—she wielded her knobby chin with the authority of a conductor's baton, pointing it now at this woman, now at that (let's hear it from the woodwinds; and now the brass). Under that crypto-direction, the women seemed to be drawn to their assigned tasks by a benign process of natural selection. Soon only Jane and Melissa remained in the hut to help Carla with the kitchen chores.

"Use the heel of the palm, like this." Jane had the muscle, Carla praised her, giving her firm upper arm a congratulatory squeeze.

"Tennis," Jane acknowledged with an embarrassed laugh. She received any woman's touch as a liberty taken, and resented as such.

"It's all in the wrist. You'll learn."

The dough was pronounced elastic enough and tenderly covered with a cloth. Melissa was making cheese from the goats' milk. It might be interesting to watch, Carla observed to no one in particular.

Jane's interest did not need to be directed to Melissa. It had been fixed on the tall blond woman since the girls had separated from the boys. In the geometry of the heart, all triangles are equilateral, the angles congruent. If not Rafe, then Rafe's wife would do. If she *was* Rafe's wife, which was what Jane meant to learn. Once the cheesecloth bag full of clotted milk was pendant, free to slowly drip into the pan below, Jane began a circuitous questioning.

"Is everyone here married? Or do you have singles too?"

Melissa looked at her soberly. How clear are her eyes, Jane thought, as if they were swimming in Murine. Perhaps there was something to this diet, after all. Not one tiny red vein in the white.

"Everyone here has taken the Vow."

"That's not what I asked. Come on, Melissa, a simple question deserves a simple answer."

"Our union lasts forever. It is indissoluble. That is the nature of our Vow."

"Okay, okay," Jane said, impatient as always with the eternal, no time for the everlasting. "But when you came here, you were married? Legally, I mean?" My wife's, Rafe had said of the dress.

"Each of us was alone. Now none of us is alone. We are joined together by—"

"Yeah, yeah, the Vow. Forget it." There was something in that voice, so persistently soft, that made Jane think suddenly of Irene. Or was it the serene constancy of her gaze? Jane did not share Boone's contempt for his sister, unmistakable even in his first acknowledgment of her.

Have you any brothers or sisters? A question of morbid importance to Jane, only child.

Just Irene. A man confessing to small means.

So Jane had expected—what? Some insignificant woman of nondescript color, unremarkable presence, forgettable face. Had met instead a flamboyant gypsy—such was her first impression of Irene, whose manner of dressing in peasant blouses and dirndl skirts heightened the illusion. Insignificant? Jane squirmed when introduced. That's me, not her. Who would not feel somewhat diminished as a woman before that overflowing cornucopia of female goodies: heavy breasts emerging like half-moons from the drawstring neckline worn far off the shoulder, hips whose sway was undisputed even under yards and yards of skirt, dark hair curling wildly into a corona, thick lashes raised and lowered like a theatrical curtain over eyes of a fuzzy velvet brown. Eyes never changing in their unfocused softness, as if in a state of permanent refraction.

That was Jane's first impression: gypsy. An image rife with stereotypical adumbrations. Golden earrings and ropes of beads. Dancing bears. Raffish colorful clothes. Swarthy lovers with white teeth. Tempestuous behavior of manic-depressive intensity. Violins playing Tchchernia and cuban heels stomping wildly.

Wrong. Absolutely wrong. The music to which this woman moved was *Parsifal*. To be in her presence was to bask in quietude. Jane had never before known a woman who sat with hands folded in her lap. To Jane it conveyed a picture of imperturbable inner grace. True, with her hands so still, her tongue clicked off a rosary of strangely assorted mystical beliefs, but how could you argue with someone whose voice was always whisper-soft, whose smile was so searingly sweet?

What does she do?

Do? Boone's face assumed a sardonic cast, a look that relegated Jane to his freshman class. "She survives."

What Irene did, as far as Jane could tell, was stand in unemployment lines. And move to new apartments, always a tiny studio up five walk-up stairs, with an alcove for the daybed, a closet for the kitchen, and a bath down the hall. Always the same thin Indian cotton bedspread, the same threadbare oriental on floors black with old varnish, each new room suffering the same diseases of decrepitude, from the psoriasis of flaking ceilings to the ascites of bulging walls.

At some time or another she must have worked, if only to be eligible for those weekly checks, but Jane never caught her at it. Equally mysterious was her ability to find those little apartments, so many of them, whose rents were as modest as the conveniences they offered, all within a ten-block radius, a neighborhood now considered highly desirable with its charming artists-in-the-attic past adjoined to a present building boom of expensive high rises.

Yet never the legal tenant, it would seem. A kind of sublet, Irene defined it vaguely, leaving even the legality of that open to question. A friend of a friend, she might further explain sweetly, and wave an arm, setting a dozen thin silver bangles tinkling, inviting Jane to inspect the premises (that one small room), a bravura gesture like the lowering of a velvet rope in a museum, throwing open a new gallery with an intricate maze of corridors to the visitors. What undulating curves in that arm. No hint of an infrastructure of bone. Even the elbow—Jane diligently creamed her own rough protuberances every night—was no more than a dimple.

She's putting on weight again, was Boone's cool response to Jane's admiration. As a brother, Boone was a disappointment. More like the brother of a brother. Poor Irene. Even her closest relative was once removed.

She had flatly denied that Irene was fat and so had begun their first bad fight. Perhaps the fact that she herself was on a diet accounted for the union militancy with which she sprang to Irene's defense. Couldn't he see that flesh, the very abundance of it, could be seductive? "As fashions go, I'll take corsets and stays over anorexia nervosa any time."

"All right, fat's the bad word, now what's the good word?" That stupid childhood game of his. "Lush, how's that?"

"Lush, okay. What's wrong with that?"

"Okay. Irene's lush. I'll settle for that." No settlement at all. A victorious sneer, as if she had fallen into a semantic trap.

Reasonable as always, Jane restricted herself to the physiological facts. Nature herself had plumped women out. Thanks to the extra layer of fat, they floated longer in water. They could wear low-cut sleeveless gowns in unheated rooms without freezing to death. Even when Boone snorted—ha! that's teleology for you, the better to hang your boobs out on a cold winter night!—she kept her cool, developed her thesis in lecture form: Women were once admired in their natural state. (Slide, please. Rubens' Garden of love.) But today men like their women skeletal. (Slide, please. Vogue models for swimwear in institutional-like shower, positioned in agony. Or is this the Buchenwald gas chamber?) Sick, sick, sick. Whenever you lecture, Boone had said with a leer, I have this old fantasy of fucking my high-school teacher. She had pushed him away. Reductio ad absurdum, she had said, having the last word, she thought, but he overrode her.

Last night too. A sudden spasm, the flesh remembering, made her grasp the counter like a Victorian maiden threatening to swoon away. Why was he good only in battle? Why did tenderness unman him so that she dared not touch him kindly or explore him gently (not there! not there! he squirmed, pumping with his palm at his ear as if she had tongued some gnat into the labyrinth) or snuggle up for childish comfort, two bodies better than one in the enormity of night?

Unmarried, she had at least the pleasure of throwing him out, timed when the logistics were in her favor, some of his things moved to her place, none of her things as yet moved to his. That first split had lasted half a year. What a stupid thing to argue about, it seemed in retrospect. Irene's weight. Lush, was the good word he had offered her. Of course, at the time she did not know that Irene drank.

"Why not show Jane the compost pile?" Carla suggested.

Melissa understood the directive. "We'll empty the garbage," she translated for Jane.

Together, with the heavy pail hoisted between them, they waddled out. Jane found it hard to match her stride to Melissa's longer one. The pail bumped painfully against her legs. "Far?" she asked, annoyed to find herself panting.

Melissa looked at her in surprise. "Here, let me." With an effortless swoop, she lifted the pail on her shoulder, one hand holding it in balance, the other akimbo on her hip. A Biblical stance. Rebecca at the well, but carrying slops, not water. Jane still had to trot to keep up.

Through the open windows of the Dome, flanging outwards like bits of skin peeled back from a monstrous globular fruit, came the exclusive voices of women. Happy sounds, laughter trilling with excitement, cleaning chores taken lightly as a holiday festivity. No loitering, move on, Melissa called back. Waited for Jane to catch up. Unfinished as it was, the Dome was used only on the Feast of Elath and required some readying, she explained, moderating her army sergeant's tone.

The shed they passed next was an eyesore to Jane's urban-trained eye. All farms seemed blighted with sagging outbuildings that, in the sternly upright parlance of the city, should have been condemned. This one, typically, seemed to be standing only because the four walls had yet to agree which way to fall. The earth in front was stained black with the oil of incontinent machines. Inside were two tractors, as formidable as tanks.

Garage and machine shop, she noted, peering into the shadowy interior as they passed—and a clubhouse for men. Their passing was no occasion for friendly chitchat—Melissa's pace saw to that—but at least the four men who came to the wide doorway, wiping oily hands on equally oily rags, smiled. Melissa did not turn her head, but Jane smiled back. And almost impaled herself on what she thought at first was the fossil backbone of the same prehistoric beast whose rutted marks she had seen in the sun-baked mud. As indeed it was, she realized; at least it was some part of the same beast, one of the several tractor attachments scattered in the grass. Scythe-like blades, dragon-toothed blades, double-helix blades—all as obscure in purpose as the jumble of oil-soaked attachments to Mrs. Caligor's old sewing machine. Mammoth ruffler? Tucker? Hemmer? She would have to ask Boone, who, if he didn't know, should be learning, future farmer that he was.

The compost heap was finally reached. Within the wired enclosure, two overalled figures were busy with pitchforks. The denim bibs gaped, revealing smooth pectorals shiny with sweat. Nice bodies, all these men, Jane approved; there was nothing like paucity of hair to give the male torso a classical cast. Too arty, perhaps? Too like female calendar nudes missing all pubic hair.

"Hi there," she said, determined to get something going on an integrated plane although the compost pile was not an idyllic spot for dalliance.

The men continued to ply their pitchforks, the rhythm of their work only momentarily broken. Their answer was monosyllabic, the look they gave her almost surreptitious. She suppressed the impulse to tap them on their hairless chests and say with painful clarity: me, Jane, you Tarzan.

"There, that's done," Melissa said, speaking only to her, as if they were alone. Swinging the empty pail, she was off again, drawing a reluctant Jane in her wake. Jane felt a hot spot on her back—were they staring at her?

"The sun," she complained, feeling too much skin exposed. She untied her shirt and let it hang loose over her jeans. "Aren't you hot?" She found it irritating that Melissa looked so cool. "Especially in that high-necked long-sleeved dress?"

If she were only willing to try it, Melissa suggested, she would find that long skirts were more comfortable than pants, creating their own breeze. Some truth in that, Jane conceded. The flapping of her shirt around her waist had brought relief. Was there a spare dress for her? She wouldn't mind trying one on. The decision was a light-hearted one, like the acceptance of an invitation to a costume ball.

The lack of mirrors in the dormitory hut was a blow to more than her vanity. The absence of her new image left her new identity obscured. Until she knew how she looked ruffled at neck and wrist, skirted to the floor, she did not quite know how to act. She curtsied—pure bravado. As if it were a model's ramp, she sauntered down the center aisle formed by two opposing rows of narrow bunks, so closely aligned, so tightly blanketed. Not beds to ever know erotic disarray. Not beds to even sit on. Sit she did—more bravado. Melissa's eyes, clear and limpid, still could convey climatic changes. Cold disapproval. Provokingly Jane fell back, sprawled languorously.

"Tell me, how do you arrange it? How does it work? One-on-one, take turns, free-for-all, catch-as-catch-can?"

"What?" Melissa asked.

Jane did not believe in that blank stare for a moment. She said it pugnaciously, a chip-on-the-shoulder word, daring Melissa to knock it off. "Sex."

Oh, sex. Melissa smiled as if a misunderstanding had been cleared up. "Sex is for two. We are one."

Jane sat up. "Oh God." She was not one to use His name in vain, only in disgust.

"I take it you are on your honeymoon? I can remember when I too thought of sex as the tie that binds man to woman, woman to man." Melissa's voice was gentle, pitying. "Dear Jane, that is something you must think about, now that you are here." Melissa showed her concern by perching precariously on the edge of the bed, taking Jane's hand, plucking at the loose back skin, making little tucks in it. From a caress, Jane would have recoiled. Pinches, she found endurable. "Sex is a sundering force, not a joining one. A fallacy. Like alcohol, which only makes you high at first, then lets you down all the harder. Be honest with yourself. Think of the last time you and your husband made love. How brief the illusion of closeness, and even then how removed from each other in your thoughts. And afterwards—" Melissa shuddered, like someone thawing before a comfortable fire who suddenly remembers the freezing cold—"afterwards were you not more lonely, not less?"

Jane grew impatient, even with the pinching. Postcoital tristesse seemed an inadequate foundation for a revolutionary life style. "Oh, sex has its shortcomings," she said and giggled nervously, "some shorter than others. But nothing is perfect."

Melissa disagreed. "We who have taken the Vow know better." She leaned closer in her earnestness and Jane drew away. Instinctive response to territorial aggression. Suddenly puzzled, Jane questioned her own senses. Even so close, there was no smell to Melissa at all. Puzzling, because Jane prided herself on an olfactory keenness, boasted that when she awoke in the middle of the night, even in that disoriented state, the smell of the man beside her identified him before she remembered his name.

Much to Jane's relief, the tête-à-tête was broken by the intrusion of a third person into the hut. Rafe stood in the doorway, eclipsing the sunlight, a corona of shimmering rainbow colors around his fair head. Surprised at finding the room occupied, he simply stood there, the biceps of his left arm tightly clasped by his right hand. A strangely inconclusive gesture, as Jane read it, midway to "up your ass" or some such colloquialism.

She rose quickly, her thoughts already maneuvering Melissa out of the picture, arranging a scene in which she and Rafe were alone in a room with a surplus of beds. Instead it was she who was evicted. Erased. Ignored even as witness to the passionate exchange between these two. The air was charged with the voltage of their unspoken thoughts.

"You were in the Dome." A statement of fact apparently so obvious Rafe felt no need to respond. "You knew the women were there, that it is forbidden once the horn has blown."

"They had finished. They had all left. I went there to fix the wiring—they had reported a short. I went to make sure the freezer was on."

"But someone was still there."

Another obvious fact, his shrug confessed. Equally obvious to Jane, yet another fact: this was the interrogation of a jealous wife. All that crap about sex as a sundering force. These two were as one, all right, both emitting the overwhelming scent of desire.

With admirable control, Melissa kept her voice dispassionate, calm. "The Windigo will know. He will be angry."

Jane could not let that pass. "Are you people really so childish? Is that what you do when you have a fight—run to Big Daddy and tell on each other? Can't you work it out between yourselves?"

They were reminded that she was there. "You do not understand," Melissa said. "The Windigo will know." Melissa was also reminded that no more time should be wasted, that she and Jane had their womanly duties to perform, whatever trouble Rafe had gotten himself into.

Jane followed her precipitate exit obediently, managing in her haste to trip on the threshold. A Freudian trip, she knew very well, that would not have occurred had Rafe's arms not been so readily available. But Rafe did not catch her, she was forced to save herself, grasping at the door jamb just in time.

The sunlight was blinding. For a moment there seemed to be no color to anything on earth. Color could not exist in that hot amalgam of white. Out of the corner of her eye, she had seen Rafe's abortive movement, his hand reach out to the rescue, only to draw back again, resume its tourniquet hold.

"Melissa, wait! Rafe is hurt, there's blood!"

Melissa did not stop. She called back over her shoulder. "Yes, I know. He can take care of that himself. We have our work to do."

Chapter IV

Unlike Rafe, The Windigo moved at a processional pace which Boone found more compatible with the vital capacity of his lungs. A cigarette, carelessly lit, was impossible to draw on with the air so heavy with disapproval. Boone flicked it away. The silence held. Boone found it surprisingly comfortable; usually with strangers he felt a need to talk, proffering conversation like a handshake, a disarming politeness to show the mind as well as the hand reassuringly empty. Admittedly, he sometimes talked too much.

You always talk too much. Jane's voice, honed to a fine critical edge. A great sulker in silence, that woman, except in his private thoughts. Face to face with him, she baffled understanding, her speech disintegrating into a Morse-like code of dashes and dots. Silences more memorable than words:

"You always talk too much . . .words, words, words . . .even when—" Dashes and dots studding the wedding night.

"Even when what?" Better chronic diarrhea than acute obstruction, he should have told her on that official occasion.

"Never mind . . ."

"For Chrissakes, even when what?"

"Never mind . . ."

Silences with barbs. Barbs that merely pricked his skin, that she withdrew without ever plunging in. And yet they hurt. Even a scratch can lead to infection. He thought of a more recent night, when he had taken her at her word, taken her without a word The silence was sweet again.

And silence suited the early morning, which seemed something to breathe in and out slowly, deeply. The heat would be oppressive at noon, but at this hour the sun's warmth on his head was as healing, as holy, as a laying on of hands. At the same time, his feet were being licked by still wet grass. He leaned over and plucked a tendril of vetch, reminded of the curling dampness of Jane's hair. He felt a need to concentrate on the minutiae of nature—say, this delicate fern-like weed, which The Windigo had identified for him with a contemptuous glance—rather than look out across the meadow to the cornfields beyond the fence. Agoraphobia, that was what he was coming down with. He could not recall having been so affected as a child. Then it was time, not space, that seemed boundless. He could only conclude that when young his vision had been shorter, even as his height, focusing at things close at hand: the locust tree beside the converted barn; the wooden silo; Uncle Eban; Aunt Flo; a little scene framed like a daguerreotype by the round window in the crow's nest atop the house. As he now stared at a curling strand of green weed. Vetch. What weed-like names they gave to weeds, names contemptuous as The Windigo's glance.

"Just how big is the farm?" As if self-addressed, the question brought home an embarrassing truth. He knew nothing about this place. "The will was a holograph, leaving me everything, but no details. The court had to appoint an executor, you see. I guess he knows what it's all about but so far he hasn't shared his knowledge with me. He agreed with you that I should come here now—it would speed up probate, he said. I meant to go right into town and see him, but this feast of yours—"

"Your uncle owned a quarter section. Those fields you passed outside the gate, we'll mark them off for you in time. All in corn, as you saw. A cash-grain crop."

Boone was grateful for the interruption. His rush of words, intended only to explain his ignorance, had been diverted into a whine of complaint, directly partly at The Windigo for imprisoning him at such a time, partly at Uncle Eban for the cavalier way he had drawn his will. All my worldly goods, ran the summary bequest, echoing the words he must have uttered a half century ago to the woman he took as bride. All my worldly goods I thee endow. As if death and marriage were the same sacrament. Odd that The Windigo had made the same connection in his eulogy. Something about marriage and hanging, Rafe had quoted at the head of the stairs. He shook down his thoughts, muddied by the vague memories of his childhood visit and the clearer, more gruesome image of Uncle Eban swinging from a rafter. Now was the time to be business-like, confirm his ownership.

"What's that in acres?"

"Hundred sixty."

"A good-sized piece of land," Boone commented with a satisfaction that evaporated under The Windigo's smile, a sneering twist of full lips cancelled by the unclouded benevolence in the dark brown eyes.

"Good-sized? No. Not in these times, not in these parts. Agri-business, they call it now, not farming. But a good size, yes, to our way of thinking. A quarter section for each family was the pattern the home-steaders cut the land by, taking what they could use, not what they could grab. At one time your uncle owned two square miles, still not what they call a big man here, but more than he could manage when he grew old. Sold off a quarter section here, a quarter section there. What you have left is a farm of human not corporation size."

Boone felt a sense of impoverishment. What he had left seemed now a garden plot. "Too bad he was childless. If he'd had a son, he might have held on." A short-lived regret. Boone had no desire to wish away this inheritance, however shrunken in his esteem.

"He was alone," The Windigo agreed. And made the first proselytizing move. "As all are alone who have not taken the Vow."

Boone quickened his pace to remove himself physically, veering toward the long low shed that yawned open just ahead. "Oh, I think he made out all right—he and Aunt Flo. They had each other for sixty-odd years." More than his mother's whole life span, Boone suddenly realized, feeling cheated in her behalf. "Not many people have that kind of marriage any more."

The Windigo, with no evidence of hurrying, was still by his side. "That kind of marriage," he repeated with a put-down smile. "A celebration of loneliness. Your uncle hanged himself, you know."

"Not my uncle. My great-uncle," Boone corrected, thus removing himself a generation's length from blame. Dad was the nephew who had not given the uncle a thought, who had enough on his hands with Mom getting worse, getting better, getting worse, getting better. Hers had been that kind of disease. Never an all-out attack, only guerrilla forays that erupted without warning in a body seemingly at peace, then withdrew as suddenly into the underbrush of flesh. A war of nerves. The thought was like a death's-head grin. Her hands as quiet as Irene's until she reached out, and then the tremor. Her head held stately with a model's poise until it turned, and then the silly bobbing up and down. Dying, dying, dying, and finally dead. A time-consuming death. No time left for an uncle, a great-uncle, who had written last some twenty years ago to invite the kids back for another summer.

A compliment, Dad said. You must have behaved yourself.

The answering scream rang out, as fresh with terror as if it had just been sounded, an acoustical freak due to some strange topography of the mind. *I won't go! I won't go!* Irene, no doubt.

Irene had been here too—he had forgotten that. She was the screamer, the kicker, the biter, at least in the good old days, although Jane would never believe it, mistaking an alcoholic daze for the peace that passeth understanding. A mistake shared by Irene, who proclaimed her rebirth semi-annually. Thanks to the Maharishi. Or Meher Baba. Or

Madame Blavatsky. Or Krishnamurti. The early morning rigors of Zen. Or the weekly ardor of a Subud latihan. Avatar of the Month. Did she get one free on joining, and build up dividends with each subsequent purchase?

Still it could be worse, was the period he always put to any thought of Irene. Worse, though never spelled out, was the specter of a five-, ten-, twenty-year analysis, and who would have paid for it, Dad already disabled by Mom's medical bills. Besides, as nuts go, she was only half-cracked, ran his defense. Plainly it could be worse, he ended now as he always ended, not unaware that he was echoing her own implied threat, not strongly voiced but faintly sighed, as when she greeted him with the silver tinkle of an odalisque's arm and a smile ferocious with renewed serenity. He knew then what was coming and the order of it: first the announcement, delivered with all the radiance of a soprano singing "Ah, Sweet Mystery of Life," that now at last she knew the meaning of it all. Then the faint sigh. Oh, Boone, I can't tell you what it was like *before*. And how can you argue with that? he shrugged in final dismissal, and came to a halt beside the open door of the shed.

"I see you are interested in machines." The Windigo did not breach the doorway, although a movement of his head gave Boone permission to enter. "We are over-mechanized for a farm this size, I'm afraid, but these are relics from your uncle's more active years. Sadly dated—antiques, in our neighbors' eyes— but with care they can be kept going for a while."

The four men serving as mechanics stopped their work to give him their courteous attention. Had he ever driven a tractor before, the man with the squashed nose wanted to know. Never, Boone admitted. The one with the curly dark hair of a poodle (Marco, Boone remembered, relieved that at least one name had stuck) slapped invitingly the flank of the larger of the two machines. Clumsily Boone hoisted himself into the seat and wondered uneasily if he had done it right or if, like a horse, the tractor demanded a certain protocol of mounting. Hanging over the side, Marco introduced him to the controls, the master clutch, the gear box regulating a confusing number of speeds. How fast, was what Boone immediately wanted to know and blushed at his own naiveté when he heard that eighteen, maybe twenty mph was tops.

"Not that you'll go *that* fast," Marco assured him, obviously biting back a smile. "Maybe on the road, getting down to the far field, but that's all."

More beast than machine. Even stationary, it made Boone aware of its power. He gripped the wheel, wanting to assert his mastery, start it up, back it out. But The Windigo must have given some sign of impatience, for Marco jumped off, his waiting stance making it clear Boone was expected to follow.

"The Windigo is waiting to show you our corn," Marco said kindly. "You're lucky, coming when you did. Once the corn is waist-high, we've nothing much to do but eye the weather. There'll be time to teach you all you need to know."

Boone was lucky indeed, a chorus of agreement assured him, each man remembering the adverse timing of his own first Feast of Elath.

"So cold I froze my ass off. And no heat in the Dome."

"For me, it had to be plowing time. I was ready to drop in my tracks."

"Harvesting is worse. And as if having to get the crop in wasn't enough, the combine broke down."

Mock complaints. An inverse kind of bragging. Faces alight with joy remembered. The way a man talks of his first misadventure with sex, proud not of the way it happened but that it happened at all.

The Windigo's mouth snapped back from its stretched rubbery smile. For these men, recess was over. Boone, playing follow the leader, picked his way over the oil-soaked stretch of ground into a long sweep of pasture. The corn—so he had been promised—was their destination. If so, there must be more than one way out of this compound; he was quite sure the gate through which he had driven was in the opposite direction.

There was a slight drag to his step, the flapping of paper stuck to the sole of his shoe. He pulled the paper off, begriming his fingers with a sticky mix of dirt and oil. Not paper, oh Lord. Oh Lord, oh Lord, oh Lord kept bubbling up, a mindless belching, Aunt Flo's special cry of shock, not his, Aunt Flo even in its tonal mimicry of midwestern flatness. A glassine envelope that size was not five-and-ten retail. It must hold a half-kilo. Wholesale, oh Lord, oh Lord. Aunt Flo, wringing her hands. Aunt Flo, wringing their necks. Memory stirred, like a child awaking in a dark room, waiting for the furniture to take shape.

The Windigo unlatched a gate, which all but collapsed once rusty hook was lifted from rusty eye. Gate within a gate, fence within a fence, this one no more than goat-high, of flimsy chicken-wire, with none of the authority of the outer linked-steel circumference. Boone blinked, almost blinded by a wild semaphoring of the sun. Glassine envelopes everywhere, like a propaganda barrage dumped from the sky. His first thought was of an accidental spill, randomly carried on the wind. Then he laughed, a sharp explosion of relief, as he considered the odds on every envelope being randomly speared by a green stalk.

"Here is our corn," The Windigo said. Boone looked hard, not understanding a voice so burred with pride. This was an overgrown vegetable patch compared to the real giants outside the real fence. No two rows were alike but in the perky wearing of those transparent caps: some low and bush-like, all but unrecognizable as corn; some ramrod straight, grossly thickened in the stalk, looking more bamboo for furniture than corn for food; yet others, in a neighboring row, so frail they buckled, leaned askew, or had in fact snapped off.

"But—but—" Boone stuttered, gesturing to the horizon—"all that corn out there, isn't that our corn?" And warned himself to be more careful about sharing possessions.

Cash grain, The Windigo reminded him as if that served to dismiss the corn out there. "A good double-cross hybrid dent, two-hundred-fifty bushels an acre it gave us last year, in spite of the drought. The local grain elevator takes it all, that's where the cash comes in." In that clipped statistical dryness of tone, the green sea that to Boone's eye flooded the earth evaporated into a speculator's abstraction. Commodity futures. Puts and calls. The Windigo's eyes grazed stolidly over the distant prospect. "One hundred twenty acres of it. A factory. A production plant." But when he refocused on the small plot before them, the change in voice was remarkable. These two acres, he said with a modesty that could only be described as false, were reserved for experimental seed corn—Research and Development was the departmental title he gave it with a chuckle that confessed it all sounded very grand.

Boone nodded, still listening to that voice. Yes, an unmistakable coyness had seeped in. Even a vibrato of sexual excitement, as if there were a pornographic salaciousness to the R & D of seed corn. The Windigo was a good businessman—the executor had written him as much. *It would not be putting it too strongly to say he saved your uncle's farm. Highest yield in the county, four years in a row, not a penny now outstanding on your uncle's loans.* That from an officer of the local bank who should know. Boone surveyed the straggly, unkempt, weirdly varying plants. Failed experiments, all. What we have here, Boone sized up smartly, is the one piece of land that doesn't make money. For a businessman, what nastier perversion?

"Those bags—" and he saw now that others of a more slender, popsicle shape protruded from the sides of the stalks—"they have something to do with your research." The answer was so obvious, he did not bother with a raised inflection.

"We will begin at the beginning. Although—" The Windigo smiled, not at Boone but at the corn—"The beginning is our end, as yet the greatest of unknowns."

The thick fingers with their spatulate tips, weathered like barnwood to a neutral color that could not be called brown or white or red or yellow, hovered over a spindly giant, untwisted a metal tie, removed the bag covering the corn's malehood. The freed tassels shook in the breeze like the golden manes of stallions. A fine dust was snorted into the air, powdering The Windigo's fingers. "As you see, an early maturing strain." He rubbed the pollen between the tips of his fingers. "*Farina fecundus,*" he murmured, holy words in priestly Latin. Then, with extended arm, open hand, he offered it to the wind. Hierophantic gesture. Or military salute.

The second more slender bag was removed from the plant's flank. Tenderly he undressed the young ear shoot, peeled back the husk. Like the tiny milk teeth of infants, still embedded in the gum, Boone thought. "The hair of the maiden," The Windigo said, stroking the delicate blond silks. Down this silken slide came the male sperm, the fecund pollen.

Boone considered the androgynous arrangement. Go fuck yourself, as more than rhetorical retort. Reprehensible conduct, he ventured to suggest, even for a vegetable. "From a genetic, not a moral, point of view, of course."

The Windigo was not amused. "The wind, the wind," he said impatiently. "In the natural course of events, the wind sees to it that there is open pollination from plant to plant." But nevertheless, he conceded, Boone was not far wrong. Was he aware that corn was unique among the Gramineae? Not in being both male and female, but in housing the two sexes separately. Hence, so vulnerable to manipulation. "Now," he said and stood back as if to uncover the mystery. "You see?"

Boone's mind made the quick leap to the glassine bags. His laugh was loose and free, for once genuine amusement, not a protective device. Condoms, that's what they were, slipped over pricks. And diaphragms cupping all-too-receptive ears. No X-rated ejaculation into the deep throat of the wind. No random begetting by indiscriminate silks. No beldam gossiping of grass: God knows who the father is!

"Family planning," Boone said, going public with the joke.

To his surprise, the phrase was solemnly received. "Family, yes. You sense the bond. That is good." The voice, gravelly as the face, rasped more harshly, calling Boone back to business. "As you see, the wind counts for nothing now. It has been phased out. An obsolescence. Scornfully he paid his compliments to the cash grain crop—new hybrids so unlike the old chancy, haphazard mix of the wind's inventing, re-inventing, yet always preserving. Seed was no longer taken from the field, it was manufactured for each new crop, from one strain thrice inbred crossed with a second strain thrice inbred, the hybrid progeny crossed again with the hybrid progeny of two other inbred strains. "As you remarked, once the wind is circumvented by these bags, then inbreeding—selfing, we call it—is easily accomplished."

And such inbreeding, The Windigo boasted—or so it seemed to Boone. How much greater than the brother-sister matings that animal husbandry must resort to. How much more quickly one arrived at the desired results. Boone was about to cavil at this—surely a clumsy, already antiquated form of genetic engineering?—when the deep voice thundered, "Desired by *whom*, you ask?" Boone was startled. *Had* he asked? "By the machine. Always the machine."

Not boasting, then. A jeremiad. A prophet's finger of outrage pointed to the green horizon as an abomination to be reviled. It was a Faustian bargain man had made to achieve such perfection of form, such fecundity of growth. He had sold corn's soul to the devil in accommodating it to the machine: the shank not too short or too long for the machine to break off; the stalk not too flimsy or too tough for the machine to pass over; the husk not too loose nor yet too tight for the machine to shuck; the number of ears no more and no less than a machine could take, growing at just the height the machine prescribed, all resistance tailored to today's weather, today's pests.

"Meanwhile so much is lost. Bred out. The old corns—the gourdseeds, the flints, the flours, the pods—vanish like the buffalo. For each choice made, a hundred other choices have been rejected. With each new generation, the seed is locked more tightly on its computerized route. That is the way to build a warhead, not grow a living thing. Soon there will be no turning back, no turning aside. And if then the weather changes? Some new and fatal infestation strikes at the root? Where then is the great mix of nature to which we can turn? How shall we recall the true genius of this corn from the few remaining fragments of its soul? Can you reconstruct from a few broken phrases in poor translation a great epic poem?"

Boone was stirred at corn considered as a poem. Yet he had to confess he found the conceit more applicable to the cash crop which was the object of such scorn than to this weedy undisciplined growth in which The Windigo took such pride. There was something else he did not understand.

"But here too—" he gestured at the plants with their bagged private parts—"aren't you playing the same game?"

"How else to reverse direction but by retracing the steps? We began just in time, while there were still remote pockets of open-pollinated corn to be found. These we inbred, yes—but backwards, choosing the most primitive characteristics to combine, to further inbreed, to recombine. Sometimes the result is monstrous. Sometimes it is sterile. We must then choose again, pass through more generations of selfing, always groping for the way back, always coming closer to the original genetic stock."

Backwards, ever backwards! The moral firmness with which The Windigo made his stand reminded Boone of Thurber's little man plowing up a hill with the banner inscribed Excelsior! A word which, regrettably, had long ago been shredded into stuffing.

The sun mounted higher. His interest wilted. But there was still another shed at the far end of the enclosure to be inspected—a metal-sided, metal-roofed structure (ratproof, The Windigo assured him) which did not promise much refuge from the heat. The decibel level of his mutinous thoughts rose to an almost vocal pitch. If he could drive a car without knowing what was under the hood—he could, he did—then he could farm without knowing the inner machinery of what he grew. All he wanted was a dog-earred manual to read in bed, cryptic instructions issued on a need-to-know basis. Don't tell me, let me ask.

What he chose to ask, of himself, was if his growing discomfort was due solely to the heat. The odor of sanctity, faintly evident throughout the farm, was concentrated here, emanating either from those eccentric corn stalks or from the squat figure that preceded him into the shed. He wanted to learn farming; he was being taught a mystique.

Irene. Sharp as the twinge of a touched nerve, the name pricked him. Irene, the lover of mysteries. Irene should be here, she and The Windigo would hit it off.

As he had feared, the heat was even worse within the shed. He made the solipsistic error of attributing The Windigo's look of concern to an appreciation of his discomfort. But it was only the seeds he had thought for, The Windigo made clear. Their viability might be damaged by prolonged heat.

"The small generator behind the shed usually keeps it very cool in here," The Windigo assured him. "Let us hope its repair does not turn out to be too complicated for my men. I should not like to have to wait until we go into town."

"I thought seeds lasted forever," Boone said, not sure that he had thought of seeds at all. "My mother used to buy those little packets in the dime store to plant in window boxes. Just this spring my sister came across some in the bottom of a drawer, God knows how long they'd been there, several years at least, but when she planted them, they came up all right." But had they come up? There had been something willful in his refusal to notice whether his mother's windows had bloomed again. Life goes on, Irene may have meant to say, but Boone would have left the narrow boxes of dirt in their hard-baked barren state—a more fitting homage, like withdrawing a great player's number upon his retirement from the game.

On The Windigo's face, a flash of amusement—like sunlight glancing off a stone. "We measure 'forever' by a different standard," he remarked. "To preserve varieties you must continually plant them out. Even in storage mutations occur, and perhaps a kind of natural selection, so that after five or ten years in these bins, half the genetic material we started with may be lost. And what is left is not necessarily the fittest for our purpose."

Once started on genetics, The Windigo showed no inclination to stop. Sullenly inattentive, Boone understood at last those students of his who attended lectures like conscientious objectors assigned a meaningless alternative service, who spent the whole period doodling their notebooks into an illuminated book of hours.

The Windigo advanced along a wall of seed bins and sliding trays. The bank of metal containers was ludicrously like his father's safety deposit vault, Boone realized. There he had appeared, upon command, a week after his mother's death. Just in case, his father said, unwilling to complete the thought, no word game played with death. As one whose assets were all liquid and evaporated accordingly, Boone had savored the new experience. The catacombs of some persecuted sect was the image that had come to mind, complete with identifying password, ritual presentation of twin keys, voices subdued in awe, Spartan cubicle into which one retired for prayer.

Here too a guarded rat-proof interior, and the same solemnity in his guide. Instead of stocks and bonds, gold trickled through their fingers as they passed from bin to bin, distinguishing seed from seed. Shallow puffy-edged kernels, shaped like flying saucers. *That's flint.* Thin long opalescent kernels, shaped like fingernails pulled from their beds. That's *gourdseed.* The hard dimpled dent rattled in the hand like a mouthful of yellow broken teeth. By contrast, the tiny white sweet seemed as delicate as the little seed pearls of a child's necklace.

"And these colored kernels?" Boone dabbled his hand in the pile of red, black, yellow and purple. "That's what we eat at the table, isn't it?"

"Ah yes." The Windigo smiled at him benignly. "I am glad to see that you are courteous enough to partake of our ritual." He would have passed on, but Boone awaited the identification. "A popcorn we have been trying to breed back to its pre-Columbian purity. And with some success, though this particular strain turns out to be sterile. For ritual purposes, we rebreed each crop."

"I see. Like mules."

Bright boy of the class, The Windigo's nod implied, and Boone found himself promoted to the trays. Pulled out, these exposed dried ears preserved in toto, cob and husk and kernel, varying from symmetrical perfection to a Quasimodo deformity. "Never judge from the looks of the ear," The Windigo warned. "This little runt may give rise to a plant twenty feet tall—"

"Little Missy," Boone murmured, finding the analogy to Jane's mother irresistible. One of those early child movie stars, he explained a little sheepishly. Faced with a still-uncomprehending look, he nudged The Windigo's memory. "Like Shirley Temple, you remember *her*." Exasperation gave a high pitch to his voice even as he asked himself why he must, like her lovers past and present, demand recognition of a long-faded bit of ephemera. As always, the thought of Jane's mother produced a blown-up still of the famous moppet's face, which only with great effort could he replace with a corrective view of the woman he had finally met.

"She was always teamed with Billy Drood," he pressed on, in spite of, because of, his inattentive audience. "Surely you remember him. His comedies are classics, you can still catch them on TV. At some ungodly hour like 3:00 A.M. of course."

As The Windigo turned away, content not to understand, Boone made an effort to fix his thoughts on pre-Columbian corn but his glazed eyes turned longingly to the door. Overalls hanging on a hook. Uncle Eban's, was his first clouded thought. Uncle Eban always kept a pair hanging there for particularly dirty chores. Even when the memory cleared—not here, but in the barn; not clean overalls like these, but an old dirty pair. He stared at the stiff new denim as at a revelation of what comfort could be, made unbearably aware of the dirt-beads of sweat beneath his collar, the underarm wetness of his shirt, the prickly heat circling his belt-cinched waist, the sticky damp itchiness of the crotch. Hot, hot, hot. Unbearably hot.

"Why not?" came The Windigo's permission, and swiftly he striped off chino pants and knit shirt. Clothed now in nothing but the high-bibbed overalls, he had to suppress a transient fit of modesty at such half-nakedness. He needed no mirror to show him the unappetizing pallor of his skin outlined on his body like indelible underwear cropped at neck and elbow. Scrawny patches of hair marred his chest; the muscles of his upper arms were slack. No match as yet for these well-built studs from whom Jane could not tear her eyes. But soon enough the sun would color him, work do its reshaping. Meanwhile, he moved loose and free and wonderfully at ease.

Only now that he himself was shirtless did he notice the distinction of The Windigo's attire. Not Society issue, not their male uniform, that loose sack of a shirt in a coarse heavy weave, plain and unbleached, pulled together at neck and wrist with a drawstring pucker, billowing loosely where not confined by pants and bib. The mark of leadership, he could only suppose. The royal purple. In his presence, we poor villeins bare the torso rather than the head.

"You have yet to see the culmination of our research," The Windigo said with mild regret. "Ah well, another time."

Released for good behavior from the stifling shed, Boone looked about him with renewed interest and still saw nothing but weeds. Missed chances. Corn manqué. He was more impressed than ever with the corn in those outer fields, to which The Windigo paid such scant attention. (Like an austere literary critic disdaining the prolixity of a moneymaker, a perennial best-seller, Boone thought with amusement.) Mere cash crop it might be, but he could appreciate professionalism after examining so many misshapen forms. In a way The Windigo could not have expected, his visit to the seed plot had been an eye-opener. Before, a peripheral vision of terror had kept him from looking steadily at those endless acres of orgiastic growth but now he could brave the view. He was eager for it.

Once through the rickety gate, leaving The Windigo to fumble with the hook, he headed toward the outer circumference of the compound with a determinedly brisk step. At best he hoped to leave The Windigo behind, at least to forestall the issuance of any counter-directions. He did not stop until he came to the linked-steel fence, outside which ran the black-top road. Beyond that, the corn began. And did not end. A different universe lay beyond that road, a world unto itself, made up of earth and air and corn and sun. A factory, The Windigo had said, but to Boone it had more the awesome energy of a vast smelter. Through the haze of heat, he saw the sun as a gigantic cauldron tipping to disgorge its molten ore into billions, trillians, quintillions of leaf-shaped molds.

The Windigo placed a restraining hand on his arm. "Machine-made, remember, not man-made. The original virtue is lost. All dignity is lost. It grows as a mindless strongman, all bulging muscle, no soul. It is that soul, Mr. Everready, we seek to recover. Illimitable possibility, not illimitable growth."

Boone brushed the hand away, reached toward the fence.

"No," The Windigo said sharply and pulled him back. "The fence is electrified."

Boone felt a surge of disproportionate anger. "And why in God's name do you do that?"

Small boys, The Windigo said. And boys not so small, he added. Teenagers. Young townspeople bored and Saturday-night drunk. The sound of the horn carried, they would know the Feast of Elath had begun. "You see, they imagine lewd dances and other quaint rituals, full of intriguing mumbo-jumbo. They would scale a fence twice that high to see. So, once the Feast begins, we post an appropriate warning and turn on the current."

It seemed to Boone a rather strong measure against so minor an offense. He said so.

"Oh come, Mr.Everready, the Feast of Elath is a feast of love. Like you honeymooners, we have simply put out a sign 'Do Not Disturb.'"

Still disapproving but not knowing what else to say, Boone left it at that and allowed The Windigo to lead him away. The quickened breeze plucked at The Windigo's shirt, felt good on Boone's bare back. Farmers had a way of exchanging inscrutable looks with the sky, he noticed. "Looks like it might blow up a storm," The Windigo said.

By the time they passed the Dome, swirling dervishes of dirt were dancing wherever there was bare yard and the few shade trees were whipping the air. Boone wished he were still by the fence, looking out into the fields, watching the great obeisance of green. Yet it was the seed plot he visualized when he closed his eyes against a fistful of dirt thrown at his face by the wind. Scruffy stalks, looking raincapped against bad weather. A reminder that however hard the wind might blow, it was but the empty ranting, the pathetic bluster of a once powerful, now impotent god.

Chapter V

Jane demanded to know how he liked it.

Boone's grunt was purely dyspeptic. The aroma of barbecued kid was still with him, no longer appetizing. More of a stench. . He lay bloated as a beached whale on the daybed and did not bother to lift the arm flung across his eyes. .

Jane asked again how he liked it. Fine, he said, shooing the question away. A far more important question—why that joyless compulsion to keep on eating? He had come to supper fancying himself lighter on his feet, clearer in his thoughts, willing to grant some value to a Spartan diet however foolish the concomitant beliefs. Not at all disappointed, as Jane had been, that the promised treat of meat had been delayed a day because of the storm, with all that scarifying lightening. Discerning a slight tilt toward conversion, he had twitted himself. So many bowls of granola down, so many bowls to go—and he too would achieve the ethereal poethood of a Shelley. Or perhaps the political sainthood of a Gandhi. At the very least, the witty longevity of a Shaw.

Continuing the joke, he had bowed his head for the renewal of the Vow, lifted it to an appalling sight. A shudder of carnivorous delight marked the ceremonial passage of meat. Up and across and down the tables, double files of teeth tearing, grinding, cracking. No sound beyond the chewing, crunching, smacking, swallowing. Glossy lips, lubricious with animal fat. Boone recalled a certain primitive tribe that performed unabashed all human functions in the public eye save that of eating. Amen, he had agreed on observing that obscenity of a meal, whereupon the platter was at last passed down to him.

Rafe had started it. A childish whine, best suited to a schoolyard scuffle. Yet at the table Boone had seen himself engaged in a duel of trenchermen, a noble jousting with knife and fork. And furthering the chivalric image, Rafe wore a white bandage around his upper arm as if it were the colors of his lady, who had tied them there with her own trembling fingers, wishing him victory, the guerdon her fair self. Boone looked across at Jane, whose greasy smile attested to her satisfaction in having meat to eat at last. Tearing into his first hefty chunk—delicious, he had to admit—he asked of his neighbor chomping stolidly at his side, "An altercation with the goats? Did the kid bite back?"

A gaffe, it seemed, to judge by the silence, the discreet lowering of eyes. Boone felt ill-bred, as if he had called attention to a natural deformity. Nothing more was said. They ate. And ate. God, but they ate. He had kept pace with Rafe until the very end—there was a mordant satisfaction in his retrospective belch—even to the final crunch of ritual corn.

"Dammit, you haven't even looked."

He sat up, hoping to relieve the pressure on his chest. "I'm looking." She expected something more, he sensed uncomfortably.

"My dress, do you like it? You were rather taken with the style, I thought. Or does it require fat blond pigtails to arouse your notice?"

"Very nice, very nice. I told you so this morning. I suppose you didn't hear." Another childish defense—the downright lie. (*Have you seen that sister of yours anywhere about, she promised to shell them peas for supper tonight. No, Aunt Flo, I guess I fell asleep upstairs.*)

Jane's deep-throated practice of a laugh warned him the lie wouldn't hold. "How very observant. I didn't put it on this morning—just for dinner tonight. But honestly, Boone,"—she must need approval desperately, Boone thought, to let it go at that—"there's no real mirror here, I can't tell."

He looked and shared her doubt. It could be the way she was standing, arms aggressively akimbo. It should have been an all-obscuring fall of cloth. Instead she was defining her waist, flaunting her hips. That pathetic starlet stance of one bent knee. To his relief, she dropped the pose as if embarrassed by his critical gaze.

"Nice," he said quickly. "I mean it. Very nice indeed."

But she would not let well enough alone. She did a quick pirouette, braked abruptly so that the skirt continued to twirl on its own. Curtseyed, simpered, dimpled. Perched on his knee, arms around his neck. Blew in his ear.

"Cut that out!" He dumped her on the floor, pumped at his ear as if suffering the effect of a sudden plane descent. "Little Missy, for Chrissake."

Jane screamed, "Don't you dare—don't you dare to ever call me that!"

He tore a pack of cigarettes from an unopened carton—so much for vows made to be broken—and curtly announced he was going out for a smoke. *Little Missy.* The sneer lasted all the way down the rickety stairs, a poor attempt to fix attention on an appropriate object of scorn. Even when he stood open to the night, feeling the hammer-blow impact of a sky ablaze with stars, half of him still lingered guiltily upstairs, viewing aghast a Jane left sitting on the floor, staring in disgust at her empty lap.

    Little Missy. She kept that insult on hold, recoiling from the deeper affront, Boone's unmistakable quiver of alarm when she perched on his knee. No overt movement, not then. A somatic, vegetative shrinking of the tissues, like the edges of a touch-me-not plant curling at a hand's approach. She had deliberately provoked the anger, the dumping, by that viper's breath in his ear. How else to extricate herself from so untenable a position?

    This was the honeymoon. And marriage lay ahead, mapped clearly now as the great Slough of Despond. The thought so disjointed her she saw no reason to ever arise. She leaned her head against the bed's iron frame and closed her eyes. A mistake. She had provided the darkness for a private viewing of old movies of the mind.

    Little Missy. A flicker on a lighted screen. Hoop-skirted darling. Whoopsadaisy. Peekaboo. A pornographic display of ruffled pantaloons. Eyes open ,she stared up at the rafters, finding there too chimeras for grim company. Ah, Melissa, she addressed those gothic shadows, there's more to be said against a good fuck than ever you, poor girl, have dreamed of. More unfortunate sequelae than a transitory sadness. First the expansiveness of body, then the fatal generosity of heart. The confessional of the bed. That ultimate seduction, the telling of secrets. Mata Hari (mascara-blackened eyes, belly-dancer gear): *Tell me, bébé, how has your clever general deployed his troops?* All that bouncing in bed but a professional maneuver of two spies intent on breaking each other's wartime code. Loose lips sink ships, is what she should have remembered. Instead, she had said to Boone, "You'll never guess." Even later, meeting Lois in the flesh, he would not have guessed. Little Missy was no Shirley Temple, whose child-face, never changing, merely ballooning as it grew, seemed designed by nature to Macy's order, a perfect float for a Thanksgiving Day parade. For Little Missy, adulthood was all the incognito she required to live her days out unrecognized.

    Billy Drood the greatest comic who ever lived? Jane had wisely let that pass. Before her time, was all she said. She knew nothing but the name. So far, so good. But there came a time when Boone's enthusiasm was too much for her to take, and she consigned all slapstick comics with child-star sidekicks to the rubbish heap of an earlier generation's bad taste. Boone felt the challenge to convert. The man was a genius, he instructed her, as great as Chaplin any day, and just as graceful. Graceful as only the fat can be, moving through air as if were water or some other liquid medium that lent his enormous weight a buoyancy impossible for landed creatures to achieve.

"He drowned, you know. In a Beverly Hills swimming pool."

"I didn't know that!" Boone was shocked. No movie buff (but for TV, he might never have arrived at this singular idolatry), he was hearing for the first time of Drood's soggy end. Incongruous, he found it; a man that fat should have floated. "When did it happen? It couldn't have made much of a splash." She groaned. He winced. "No pun intended."

"None taken," she said. "God, it was years ago. In the 40's, thereabouts. I doubt if much notice was paid, with a war on. Besides, as a comic he was already dead."

She caught herself knowing too much about the life and death— she who had professed to know nothing but the name. No need to worry. Boone, the zealot, found her ignorant enough. Could it be she did not know those films? He scanned the listings of the midnight, the post-midnight movies, until he cried out. "Hot damn! Every night this week. Wouldn't you know, it's at three A.M."

I suppose you would't consider getting a VCR, she suggested weakly, knowing in advance that he wouldn't. (A matter of principle, he had haughtily explained, using strangely Luddite arguments for one who sported such a multi-functional watch.) On second thought, she was glad he was a man of principle. Were he to tape them, those films would be played over and over—a far worse fate than watching once, no matter how late the hour. So side by side they sat up in bed, covered in white sheeting below the waist, naked above, like a Pharaoh and his queen, even to that royal gesture, one arm angled across the breast holding the ureus, symbol of godhood—the remote control.

At such a hallucinatory hour, the film seemed to jump from frame to frame—a slide show for Boone's accompanying lecture on the comic art. "You never see the early ones on TV—the shorts—but they're the best. Without the kid. Sometimes there are private showings at a film club, I'll watch for that, so you can see how beautifully he wings it: no script, no plot. Best of all, no sickening child. Too bad he was ever sold the idea of doing this nineteenth-century children's classic, Little Missy. A boffo at the box office, and from then on out it was always Little Missy and Drood Together Again! Still there are some great scenes even in Little Missy— worth staying up for—trust me, hon."

Billy Drood all week. Glumly Jane resigned herself to a festival. There he was, a dirigible held to earth by the tenuous mooring of his tiny feet. Little Missy could not be far behind. The heart-shaped face with the luminous eyes of childhood—incredible!—exactly as envisaged for Gerber's baby food—wavered before her like a blur of ectoplasm summoned at a séance. Slyly she closed her eyes, letting those black and white pinpricks of ghosts cavort solely for Boone, the foolish believer, the credulous sucker, who would tell her later what wonders the medium had evoked from that other world.

Jane could not decide which was worse—to watch the little moppet single-handedly run the whole damn plantation (aided and abetted only by the joyful jigging slaves) or to close her eyes and watch herself as child watch that child.

"A disaster," Boone groaned in the brief respite filled by two middle-aged women referring obliquely to bowel movements. "Just hold on, hon. The best scene is coming up—the fencing duel with scythes, where Brood manages to run himself through from the rear." A terrible thought occurred to him. "Unless they've cut it—" They hadn't cut it. She watched yet once again lovable bumbling Massa Papa unknowingly entertain, inadvertently capture the Union spy . . .

It was not until the third night—awakened not by a sudden ejaculation of sound from the TV but by a sucking on her breast that set off a long spluttering fuse of delight—that she lost all sense of discretion. Slippery as greased pigs, their bodies lay together in after-ease.

"Damn it!" Boone cried, "we've missed the first half of *The Taxi Brigade!*" Unable to find the remote in the jumble of sheets, he tottered to the set and turned it on by hand.

With no conviction, Jane called on God. He having (as usual) failed her, she grabbed Boone's pillow, buried her head, as if that would keep Little Missy out. But the sound track cued her memory. The images it evoked could cut through flesh and bone, polyester down, the thin membrane of eyelids, no matter how tightly drawn. The little girl skipping in awkward jerks on cobblestone. A pout like the sucking on jujubes. The slow trickle of a measured supply of glycerin tears. She heard the child laugh—a stolid reading of the line ha! ha!—and could take no more.

"Hey, leave that on!" Boone's fierce protest had been preceded by the snort of a man rudely awakened from sleep.

Jane held her ground, blocking from his view even the last great sucking in of light. "I've had it with that little gamine routine."

"This part coming up is where Drood tries to slice the bread like a French peasant. Turn it back on—"

Instead she pulled the plug, as if to disconnect herself forever from that paradigm of little-girl cuteness.

"Hey, what's with you?" The question held more combativeness than concern.

"What's with me?" On yet a higher pitch, "What's with *me*?" Marking time, thinking what to say, what not to say. Not to say, that's my mother, goddamit, I've been seeing Drood and Little Missy Together Again since the age of two. Nursed and fondled, diapered and fed on that deadly mix of cutsie-pie and derring-do. "What's with you? How can you watch that shit?"

Boone stares. Boone laughs. She feels the hot flush in her face, sweat at the hairline, ice-cold fingers and toes, the arrhythmia of terror. This is the old nightmare re-released. She is naked in the spotlight. But she must perform. With no breasts and bare behind. Boone laughs. The crowd roars its animal cry of approval. She will win the Academy Award for a tap dance without shoes. She has her acceptance speech ready: All that I am I owe to Little Missy. Comes Lois on stage to tap dance beside her. Lois, six feet tall but still in pantaloons. Curtseys, simpers, dimples. Says, me too.

Twice Jane opened her mouth to tell him. Twice his laughter extinguished the truth. "What's so funny?" she managed to ask.

She was, according to Boone. She looked as apoplectic as Billy Drood. And "shit" reminded him—oh, what a joy that scene in *Gaslight Jenny*—he envied her virgin viewing of it yet to come. What an artful delivery of a hack political speech. "There he is, a poor dumb Mick, fronting for the Tweed Ring, accepting the nomination. Oh, a gem of a speech, Jane! Such beautiful oil-slick oratory! Rising to a glorious diapason of patriotic gobbledegook! He points at the flag and we're ready to hear it: *This, it is said by my worthy opponent, is the last refuge of a scoundrel; then a scoundrel I must be, for that dear flag is more to me than life itself*, etc. etc. At least, that's what he's supposed to say, he's been coached in it for days, so we know how it goes. But he gets no farther than *This, it*—when he sees Little Missy coming down the aisle, waving a placard lettered in her cute dyslexic scrawl. He can't get the words out. *This, it—This, it—This, it*—he stutters and starts over and stutters and starts over, and of course each it gets closer, always closer to *This shit, This shit*, yet the beauty of it, Jane, is that he never says it, see, he pulls up just short, so that we say it *for* him, don't you see?"

So she reminded him of Billy Drood. Vanity cried foul. Pride said, better than reminding him of Little Missy, you fool. As if that fat persona had indeed taken over, she was suddenly endowed with the grandiloquence of a carnie shill—she whose customary argument was the glowering look. From her mouth flowed a rodomontade on sexual politics, as evidenced by all films starring fat comics and little girls. Didn't Boone see what all those Little Missy movies added up to? Could he have failed to notice that ever-recurring "and a little child shall lead them" theme?

"There she is, with her baby lisp, saving England from the Armada—"

Boone could not suppress a joyful cry: "Remember Drood on shipboard? What a Sir Francis Drake! Oh, those naval maneuvers!"

"—saving Paris from the Boche—"

"That wild taxi drive to the Marne!" Boone flailed the pillows.

"—saving the Revolutionary Army, comforting the troops at Valley Forge—"

"That boat crossing of the Delaware, with Drood at the oars!" The first time he saw it, he laughed until he cried.

Impassively she waited out his reprise of laughter. A transient epileptic fit her patience replied. "Look at how all those movies end. Who gets knighted by Queen Bess? Who gets bussed by Marshal Foch? Who is commended by the father of his country? That fat blubber of a Drood. Moral: no matter what a woman does, she remains a cute and cuddly child. No matter what a woman does, some man will get the credit."

Those movies were made in the thirties, times have changed, Boone pointed out. Fashions have changed, was her snappy comeback, not the times. His irritation grew. Was it just she, or women as a group, that it was impossible to satisfy? If he might be allowed to reduce the argument to the ad hominem level (his tone now was that of an eighteenth-century gallant asking permission to take snuff), surely she would admit he had always treated her as if she were his equal?

"Aha! *As if!*" She ran him through neatly with that shrill cry. Then knowing she had him, sank immediately into Little Missy cuteness. "Methinks I heard the subjunctive case?"

"Mood, not case," came his riposte. "Faulty grammar doth faulty logic make."

Their laughs collided, a mutual admission that they were getting off the point. Anger had its labyrinthine ways, she discovered, from which emerging she saw not one but two naked men in bed. A diplopic vision. The Boone first seen with a stranger's eye (such ordinary good looks, Jane as stranger had judged him nicely) was propped against the pillows, laughing up at her. But propped on the same pillows, laughing too, was an extraordinary man with his own intensity of gaze. It was the slightly wider than usual space between the eyes—what a relief to finally figure this out—which gave him the wondering look of a primitive tribesman staring into an explorer's camera.

"Come back to bed." Boone held out his arms, peremptory with the renewed demands of sex. Boone held out his arms, confessing to emptiness while she stood there.

Panic seized her. The two Boones were merging, as if her eyes had uncrossed, the one-and-only face coming out on top. She refused to allow it. A cheap effect. Crystallization, Stendhal called it. The smooth flat planes of habit meeting in the sharp edges and corners of sex. It glitters like a diamond but on appraisal turns out glass. Will the true Boone stand up? Yes, you there. The ordinary man with the ordinary good looks. The kind of face one would be hard put to describe to the police.

A memorable moment, when the question framed itself: Is this love? If yes, why were they always reading each other out of their lives? If no, why were they always coming together again? Parting is dying—those French again. The French were wrong. Not death but a dismemberment. They parted, and pieces of Boone lay all about. His head, turned away, whizzed by in innumerable cars. His cocky walk, like a sailor's on shore leave, was assumed by someone else's legs crossing the street. His voice—a mid-sentence snatch—rang out above the cacophonous chatter in theater lobbies. She had not been shaken by such reminders; they occasioned only a mild surprise. How odd to remember the parts so well of one so undistinguished as a whole.

They came together yet once again because she had seen him a block away, had called out his name in mindless glee at knowing him from such a distance, from just the back. Boone! she had shouted, like some hysterical quiz-show contestant coming up with the right answer to the big-money question.

He had come back a block to say "Jane!" and look embarrassed. Without looking at his left hand, she was immediately aware of the wedding ring. She felt a queer twinge of gratified pain, like that from tonguing a canker on the gum. Then saw to her surprise the same strange serpentine design, the same loose fit. In other words, the same old fake.

Ah, but you're married, early on she had protested, although already rather late in the game. Sexual harassment, he had the nerve to complain. As a young male professor at Godwin, one of the last of the breed of all-woman colleges, he found it useful to signify that he was "taken." I feel for you, she had said. My heart also bleeds for the rich paying all those taxes. Not his idea, he was quick to disclaim, his sister's—

Irene's. *She* had suggested it, had pooh-poohed his objections, gone right out and bought the damn thing.

In the middle of their first argument (having just bedded), there was Irene. And Boone, laughing. Already convinced it was not funny, she asked what the joke was.

Irene, he hastily explained. What she said when she made me put it on. You'll see, she said, it'll keep all those nubile maidens at bay. And then she said, don't you worry, you'll still make out. No one pays attention to wedding rings. And he let out a whoop: that's my Irene!

Not very funny, she had said. Loose as it was, she had the ring off his finger before he knew what was going on, tossed it out her window. It really didn't fit, she said.

She still didn't find it funny. Even less funny that he must have scoured the sidewalk and the gutter to retrieve it the next morning. "You're at the university now," she said. "Do you still have to wear that thing?"

He looked so abashed, she was afraid for a moment he was going to tell her it was real. But all he could offer as an excuse—pulling it up, pushing it down over his knuckle—was that he was used to it. She took an obscure pleasure in the fact that it would never fit.

"Are you still going with that tall guy?" he asked after a moment of vacuous grinning. She must have looked as if she were twirling through a rolodex file of tall guys (where had he seen her with Alan? she was wondering) for he prompted, "Alan—isn't that his name?"

One of those Boones she had been seeing, one of those bits and pieces stuck in her peripheral vision, must have been the real Boone after all. How gratifying to have been seen with a man who—only literally, alas—towered above the crowd. Even more gratifying, Boone knew his name. He must have asked around. His interest in her was not dead. A habit of discretion—to no one had she confessed the nature of the Alan fiasco—had survival value, she now realized. Oddly enough, she had observed a stronger-than-usual caution in describing this new lover to friends, almost as if a tall and handsome and well-heeled suitor were a step down in the social scale. A sweet guy, she had said, thus distinguishing him from Boone without giving anything away. "Sweet," like "nice," was a taffy word that could be pulled into any kind of shape. Engagingly shy, she had shortly added, a man of few words (and those sweet nothings) being welcome relief. Came her final report, she was equally vague. Just not my type, wrapped it up fine. That he was a mere fill-in until the real thing came along she had known from the beginning. But then so, presumably, was Boone.

"Oh, Alan," she said now. "A sweet guy, but—" the shrug conveying that she had yet to learn how to contend with such amiability.

She was at eye-level with Boone's mouth, which (when silent) she had learned to trust more than his large-with-wonder eyes. It was there she looked for clues to his mood—a mouth loosely petulant or primed for laughter or with that peculiar set by which she knew a lie was coming. But never, thank God, with that brackish sweetness which had made a fool of her where Alan was concerned.

Boone's smile, by lifting a bit of dry lip stuck to an eyetooth, was turned into a snarl, deploying a tiger's fang. He's as nervous as I, Jane thought. Warned herself not to be taken in by mere twitches.

"A real sweet guy," she reaffirmed. By fixing her memory on Alan's courtship, her sole experience with male maneuvering worthy of that name, she achieved an elegiac tone. What would she like to do, where would she like to go, what would she like to see—her wish was his command. (Remembering now in counterpoint the last time she and Boone had decided to take in a movie they had hovered on a street corner for half an hour arguing over which to see until, holding limp wrist to his nose as if time were a scent, she had shown by her watch it was too late for either film. Trust Boone to parry with his digital read-out, according to which her watch was fast. Her watch was always fast, he reproved her, why did she have this thing about moving time ahead, like one of those street-corner salvation mongers shouting "It's later than you think!")

But at this moment, Boone's eyes were credulous as a child's. "Sweet, hmm?" he said thoughtfully. "Can it be the bad word is a bore?"

Jane bristled at the presumption, savored Alan's sweetness all the more. Like Boone, no gambler, yet he took her to the race track with no prolegomena of dark forebodings, no pitying look such as Boone/Daniel Deronda never failed to give her/Gwendolyn Harleth as she took the first step to perdition by placing a small wager at the $2 window/the gaming tables at Baden-Baden. Sweet Alan, hooraying when she won, consoling when she lost, placing her bets, fetching her snacks, and never once questioning her "system." Driving her back through day's end traffic, singing 1940's show tunes, never once pointing out that five hours work at minimum wage would have netted more than her small gains. As if money earned could ever satisfy a gambler's need. "What have you got there— four dollar bills and some loose change?" Boone would scoff at her delight. But four dollar bills and some loose change were treasure enough—had it not come, like a mother's love, expressly unearned, in no way deserved? At least she was Fortune's child.

She had a devilish urge to make much more of Alan, tall Alan, sweet as pie. Some day she would, once memory had expunged all that nastiness at the end. As it was, something within her still shrank away, curled up, felt unclean. Better settle for a bore. She ducked her head, rueful acknowledgement that Boone had hit it right on the head.

She looked good, Boone then told her. He looked good too, she served it back. Having thus expressed surprise that neither had aged (four whole months they had been apart), they walked on together, finding it easy to adjust their strides. . . .

And ended up in bed, watching Little Missy on TV.

"If you really want to see it, I'll turn it back on."

"No, if it really upsets you, we'll leave it off."

Boone settled the sheet about her with a tenderness beyond the call of sex. For that a certain trust had seemed his due. Or perhaps she merely liked to play the guessing game. The one light was on his side of the bed, she reached over to turn it out and with the cunning of a Rumpelstiltskin asked for Little Missy's name.

"Her real name?"

"Real or fancied. Nom de plume, nom de guerre. Any name, legal or assumed."

Oh yes, Rumpelstiltskin. Mean and dwarfish humor. She snickered as he struggled to recall what did not exist. There was no name. Only an eponym. *Introducing Little Missy!* was the only credit on that first film. *Played by Little Missy* followed ever after.

"You'll never guess," she taunted, tweaking the hair on his chest.

"Don't tell me!"

She told him. He turned on the light, stared at her. "Lois Mayhew?" Boone at a loss for words, imagine that. "Lois *Mayhew?* Your *mother?*"

Little Missy a mother, anybody's mother? She was asking him to accept some Ripleyesque obscenity (like those six-year-olds, always from a remote jungle village in South America, who gave birth sporadically in supermarket tabloids). She pulled the sheet up over her breasts, for he was staring as if afraid the issue was as monstrous as the act.

Boone saw it as funny, once the shock had passed: she, Jane, the full-grown woman, watching her mother, the little girl.

She, Jane, was not amused. Boone made comforting sounds. Called it a strange reversal of roles. The ultimate unnatural act. "Poor baby, no wonder they make you queasy, those films."

Oh, queasy was the word, all right. Jane felt a thrill of gratitude that Boone understood so well.

"Do you know, I can't remember a single birthday party when I didn't puke?" Too much cake was Daddy's diagnosis. Too much Little Missy was the bitter truth. Every birthday, every goddam birthday starred Little Missy and Billy Drood. "Why, why—" she beat the question against her lover's breast—"couldn't Daddy see I hated it? That Lois hated it too?"

Poor Lois, Jane acknowledged. So tiny—oh, the cuteness of it!—for so long ("Would you believe that she was twelve when *The Taxi Brigade* was made?"). Those goons in the front office were dancing in the aisles: theirs was the hottest child-star property ever—a dwarf! Even her puberty was delayed. At thirteen—if only she had the snapshots with her, Jane would show him—Little Missy still swam in topless bathing suits. Nothing. Absolutely nothing.

A little slow-witted, was that the problem with Lois Mayhew, child-star to the nation? Would another kid—a kid who couldn't act, who wasn't all that pretty, who was just tiny cute—have realized sooner the secret of her success? A whole career built on lack of size. That was why the world clutched her to its heart, why strong men wept and motherly women smiled when Little Missy blew a kiss (that sticky gesture, like pulling out an invisible strand of chewing gum) or, in a quandary of plot, swept back her straight black hair (more like a shooing away of invisible gnats) or stared uncomprehendingly at disaster (the eyes *were* luminous, Jane had to admit). Who could resist such a miniaturization of female charm?

Still better late than never; at some point in her thirteenth year, the child-star did catch on. She grew a whole foot in one year, Jane bragged, offering Boone the fact of such phenomenal growth not as a gene-set event but as a desperate effort of her mother's will. Too busy building muscle, elongating bone, to find the time to bleed, until almost six feet tall, not yet fifteen, she knew she had escaped forever the Barnum and Bailey freakishness to which Little Missy owed her fame.

But enough of Poor Lois. Jane reverted to Poor Me. "At least *she* could hide in the kitchen when Daddy set the projector up, rolled down the screen. She would suddenly remember she had to put the candles on my cake. I had to sit there in a front-row seat, the birthday girl, enjoying my special treat."

Not so understanding Boone, after all. Wholesome entertainment, he called it, none of this sex and violence stuff. Billy Drood was a natural for the kiddies, he would have thought and looked judicious: as childhood traumas went, hers merited only a C. She could see him pencil in the grade, returning her life story with the crabbed notation: re-do. His judgment, when issued, awarded damages to Lois, not to her.

On the other hand, take *his* mother. (Jane gave a silent reading of Little Missy's ha! ha! of a laugh. One by one she handed Boone the jagged cut-outs of her memory and he set to work putting together the puzzle of his own life.) He rather envied Jane those movies of her mother as a little girl. There was no such convincing evidence, he complained, that his mother had ever been a child. Nothing, not even a snapshot, taken in her youth. Unless you count a passport photo, he added with a bitterness that outdid hers.

He doesn't listen, Jane had thought. But he had listened—enough to know just where to stick the knife, how to twist it in the wound. Jane rose from her crouch, feeling a sudden hypotensive dizziness. It did not help to remember at that ill-chosen moment Lois's screech: "You're getting *married?*" Surprise appropriate to an announcement that Jane was scheduled for the next NASA flight into space.

"And why not?" Jane had challenged her mother.

"I never thought you would feel the urge," Lois said. "I always thought you were cold." Added quickly, with a grimace of distaste at being forced to use a dirty word, "Not what they call frigid—I didn't mean that. But here—" She tapped her chest, a gentle auscultation giving off a muffled thud, proving the space was occupied; daring Jane to do the same and not come up with the hollow ring of the Tin Man in *The Wizard of Oz.* "That's not a criticism, dear. Better to have no heart at all than be all heart, the way I was." That was enough to send Jane skipping down the aisle to stand before the Wizard who had performed a magic trick, endowing her with a genuine, authenticated by the document to which he had thereunto set his hand and affixed his official seal, valid until recalled, heart.

You may kiss the bride. She opened her eyes. Wrinkled her nose. Boone was over-deodorized. She smiled at the photographer. Was this a one-time event, this dousing himself with scent? Or had he acquired a new habit to set her nose on edge? Or—a thought so depressing she immediately dismissed it from her mind—had he always smelled like that?

Her father kissed her, smelling quite properly of nothing but gin. "Your mother should be here," he said. "She's carrying it too far."

Jane nodded happily at her friends. A woman, all heart, could be expected to carry it too far.

Feeling like a jumper safely landed after free-fall, but hobbled with a still billowing chute, she stuffed her yards of white satin into the car. Boone stuck two fingers between his collar and his neck. "Damn that Irene! I saw her throw it. More like hailstones than rice," he griped, and fished out a little chocolate pellet. Into Jane's lap fell a red one, a green one. Chocolate too. Jane hooted with laughter. "Don't worry," she gasped, "it's a non-fertility rite." Premarin, color-coded for potency.

Now, if only pricks were too. Alone in the barn, having pulled the second bed to a conspicuous distance, Jane couldn't stop laughing.

Chapter VI

In the immensity of the prairie night, Boone felt orphan-forlorn, ready to confess a sneaky sympathy for those flat-earth theorists who refused to balance like a trained seal on a spinning ball. He stared back at the stars, rejecting another cosmic serving up of impotence, the universe cutting him down to size.

He felt small enough—Jane saw to that. The job description of a wife? Small and very much the child—The Windigo effect, a nice added touch. Locked gates. New table manners to be learned. That windy catechesis in the corn. Locked gates. As if he were here not by his own free will but by stern parental order, the boy again, packed up, sent off, inspected at the other end for any damage to the parcel.

His father had made it sound as wholesome as cooked cereal in the morning. There's nothing like fresh air and country living, said that powerful figure, effulgent in summer shirting, as he hoisted the boy's duffel bag onto the luggage rack. Exactly what he had said the night before when Boone announced he didn't want to go. To which he had added (Boone's mother venturing to suggest ten was too young, a great-uncle and great-aunt too old) that it would be a valuable learning experience. None of which had made four weeks on a farm sound like much of a vacation.

How I Spent My Summer. For that year, the page was all but blank. Yet let him think of other years and memories multiplied thick as fruit flies breeding in the lab. Good Humor trucks, stickball in the streets, firecrackers in the park, hand-to-hand combat with stinging wet towels along the slippery edge of city pools, the jerky start-and-stop wending homeward from the beach on traffic-jammed Sundays. Those were the proper treats of summer.

For him that childhood trip, his first away from home, had been an interplanetary journey. Even now the remembrance seemed a lunatic recounting by some crackpot claiming to have been abducted by a UFO. A world of purple trees and yellow sky. Weird beings with metal objects sprouting from their heads.

The haze of memory suddenly cleared. Boone had a hard-edged picture of steel-grey hairpins popping out of steel-grey hair. Aunt Flo, whose nervous tic it was to reach a hand up, stick them back in. And Uncle Eban wore a porkpie hat indoors and out. And Irene—he kept forgetting

Irene had made the journey too—raced him from supper table to back parlor for possession of a high-backed cane-seated rocking chair. As the more practiced sprinter, he always won. And Irene always yelled.

"He kicked me in the shins!" she bad-worded him.

"You tried to trip me—I was just getting out of your way," his good-worded description of the same event. That was the evening's entertainment, to strenuously work the rocker back and forth, almost reaching the speed of take-off, while Irene sulked in an ordinary unmoving chair.

Another kind of entertainment was Aunt Flo's and Uncle Eban's: picking him apart, vying with each other at finding fault. (It showed they cared, Aunt Flo explained, when he broke down and cried. Politeness was for strangers, loving mayhem for one's kin.)

Don't tell me that's all you eat at home, you'll never reach a full man's growth. Don't tell me your ma just packed you shorts, bare legs won't do for walking through them fields. Don't tell me you just had your hair cut, you'll be taken for a girl. Don't tell me you don't go to church—

"Don't tell me you're getting married." Irene's nervous titter of surprise. In her eyes, some awful reproof. As if, falling to her death from a great height, she looked back at him, partner in a suicide pact, who refused to jump.

"Don't tell me that stink is just your aftershave," Jane carped. Never had a bride looked so chaste in motel bed.

Wrapped in paper grained like leather, boxed in simulated cork, bedded down in ersatz straw, the amber bottle bore a macho label. Attribution not in doubt. To Boone, from Jane on the gift tag below a stocking-capped rubiginous Santa.

"Our first Christmas," he had acknowledged sentimentally before the unwrapping.

"Not really our first," she corrected, kissing back. "Don't you remember when we met?"

"That's right, December 7, St. Nicholas' Day." A very Nederlandische affair, given by an ex-girl friend, ex-Southern Baptist, now married to a KLM pilot and intent on propagandizing all things Dutch.

Another redactive kiss. "December 6, darling. The seventh is Pearl Harbor Day."

They knew each other only in the biblical sense, that exchange of gifts—darling to darling—made embarrassingly clear. She laid aside her designer knee-high socks with a gesture that implied permanent discard, a sorting out of contributions to Good Will (he was to learn she considered her knees too knobby to be ever so exposed). Yet she bridled at his own non-receptive look. Asked what was wrong with men smelling good, they had a right. You've come a long way, baby, was his caustic thought before kindness settled in and he thanked her for a gift misguided but of good intent.

Jane was not satisfied—an early sign, that, which of course he missed. She scanned him intently, no doubt wondering if his distaste for manly odors betrayed too conventional a bent. She eyed his hair, perilously close to crewcut, and he knew his voting record was being questioned. Be open-minded, she urged him, as if passing him his first joint. Was it so different from an aftershave?

His doubtful look remained. The act of shaving was for Boone a chore, no ritual resonance there. Face-to-face with his own reflection, he was the one who turned aside his gaze, backed down, looked away—and wound up with a nick or two. Only when so wounded did he use a bracing lotion, applied like iodine on childhood cut, purely prophylactic in its sting and in its smell. He would have preferred to scrap the razor, to let it all hang out from scalp and chin and cheekbone; unfortunately, whenever he attempted any variation of such hirsute chic, he broke out in a rash, allergic to the sweat trapped by his hair. His father thought it funny: "I should have known. You were the only kid I ever heard of who almost died of diaper rash." Hence his unvarying close-cropped tonsure, to which he attributed the trauma of his college years, when Hair continued to make a statement, if no longer ranting wild, then simpering with bleach and permanents, or turning punky with mousse. At the least, his peers used a blower, he not even a comb. That was enough in the semiotics of the day to brand him as politically conservative, sexually inhibited, morally square. A revival of phrenology, only with character revealed not in the bumps on the skull but in the nakedness of the nape.

"Come on, just smell—" Jane dabbed a drop on the inside of her wrist, held it to his nose.

Boone sniffed with the olfactory gusto of a hound. "Boots . . . jockstraps . . . machine oil . . . fresh sawdust . . . and, yeah, something else . . ." he twitched his nostrils . . . "a recently fired gun—am I right?" He slapped the stuff on, metamorphosed into a mythical beast, half bull, half football pro, and with a bruising tackle, not forgetting the passionate snorts, pinned her on the bed. A good laugh was had by all. Sexy smell, Jane called it then, sorting out their underwear.

In the officialese of marriage, a stink.

We are virgins all, until we marry. The thought seemed to be expelled from lungs, not brain, dolorous as a sigh. Two years of living on-and-off with Jane had seemed sufficient underwriting for a marriage. He had read the prospectus. A safe enough investment. Modest but guaranteed returns. They would not take each other by surprise.

His mistake, he now admitted to the night. Boot camp training was not the same as being under enemy fire. The wedding itself was a surprise. The unfamiliar church, to which neither belonged (it was the pre-Revolutionary graveyard with which, in passing, Jane fell in love). Ushers, flowers, bridesmaids in rainbow colors—all the makings of a Busby Berkley musical except for a decent score. He could hardly make out the features of the bride-figure coming down the aisle. All the drama was in the gown, all the glory in the veil. He felt himself equally faceless, his self stopped like a clock.

But were not all rites sacrificial, processing the individual into a Jungian Velveeta, while sending up a great hurrah for group identity, the collective unconscious, survival of the race? Boone is dead, Jane is dead, long live man and wife! You may kiss the bride. Under the nimbus of white, Jane's sallow face was offered up, as lifeless as the Baptist's on a platter. Boone gave the obligatory salute, and tasted annoyance on Jane's dry lips. The woman, at least, should be satisfied. His plan had been to stop at City Hall, more or less on the way out of town. Just another item on the closing-out list. Something like: return key to landlord; get married; fill up with gas. And at first even that had seemed more ceremony than suited Jane, who agreed to the "piece of paper" with a shrug, as to a visa or a passport required for crossing borders. It was after that visit to her mother that Jane revised her stand.

"If we're getting married, let's do it right."

No ifs for Boone; Boone had made his mind up. He had certain anxious dreams, but "I can never remember dreams" he always said when Jane told hers. One he did recall. Surely he had walked down this aisle before, was his first thought when they entered the church of Jane's capricious choice—to case the joint, as she put it with a giggle. Yes—the dream was retrieved with a great sucking plop, like something fished up from lake-bottom ooze—he was walking down such an aisle as this, called up from the audience by a magician on stage. He mounted the steps, smirking like a lottery winner, to confront that turn-of-the-century poster face. Marvello, ready to astound. Step this way, please, said the lushly curved assistant in spangled tights. Boone obeyed. The transparent box

(Lucite?) was promptly locked, submerged in water. A drum roll marked Boone's descent. The assistant extended her arm triumphantly. The arm began to shake. The clock began to tick. Her head bobbed up and down. Boone screamed, "I can't get out, the water's coming in! Goddamn it, you forgot to tell me how it works! Goddamn you both, show me the trick!" Marvello tapped on the tank with his magician's wand. "That's the bad word, Boone, now the good word, please."

The dream was thrown back—a slimy catch squirming on the hook just long enough to be identified as inedible. Looking about him, Boone had visualized the wedding as Jane then planned it, and offered an opinion.

"What do you mean 'stupid'?" Jane, growing thinner by the day, had the blindly beatific look of one who had found religion in the terminal stages of a disease.

"We don't belong here," he said sharply. But that was the whine of the disinherited, the sneer of the dispossessed. He should have been brought here as a child, Boone was thinking, now it was too late. God-manners, like table-manners, were best learned at an early age. He pictured a congregation composed of men in vested suits, women in hats. Gloved hands reaching for the prayer books, opening at just the right page. Knife-pleated trousers hiked over the knee before kneeling on the maroon plush rests. He envied the assurance of their high-church devotions, not their faith, much as he envied the rich the assurance of their high-living, not their wealth. His own assurance was of a brassy, autodidact make, not worth a damn in a setting such as this.

"It's like incense," Jane said, squeezing his arm, "this smell of tradition. I knew it would be like this when I saw that little cemetery. Some of the stones are so old there's no inscription left."

They toured the rectory garden, a small gap of Episcopal greenery in an otherwise solid wall of Pentecostal slum. "This is the original brick back here," Jane pointed out, "that Greek Revival front was just tacked on."

Tradition all the way, was how Jane played it. Somehow she wangled the bishop himself to perform the service. No deletion, not one word altered in the service, she insisted when they were informed (like criminals being read their rights) that young people nowadays could write their own. "He looks like a bishop," Jane approved the Greek Revival face, while Boone observed the crumbling brick behind. Grey hair bushing out below the ears, a broad-faced handsomeness half-obliterated by the desuetude of age. "More like William Jennings Bryan," Boone said, "a seeker after high office, defeated thrice." They sounded as if they were typecasting a play. And they were married by a cleric performing in one, joining two strangers in holy matrimony with such familiar fondness it must have been assumed he had dandled them as infants at the baptismal font.

Ah, to write his own! A wiser Boone, walking his land by night, revised the sacrament on the spot. A mixed-media event. Echoes of Monty Python. Behind the altar a huge screen on which to flicker a continuous sequence of cartoons, drawn in that fine-line, pen-and-ink draftsman style, as meticulously exact as a patent application. Two disembodied heads take form—one with a Little Missy simper, the other frozen in the bug-eyed apoplectic double-take of Billy Drood. Dearly beloved, the bishop begins, and so does the action on the screen. Screamingly funny. Heads kicked like footballs, squashed with sledge-hammers, cleaved with axes, fired like rockets. Heads reaming out cannons, traversing the T's and S's of sinuous plumbing, rolling through wickets, plopping down chimneys. Enter Boots. Heads stamped on, tamped down, leveled even with the ground, while the bishop pronounces the two heads one. It is done. The invited guests rise. But wait. The punch line is yet to come. The words, wraithlike, ribbony as smoke, are visible in the air, like a message farted from a plane or writ by the moving finger of God. And Now for Something Completely Different . . .

Boone stumbled over a hillock of tough matted grass, took his bearings from the dark hemisphere of the Dome, and had a moment of vertigo as he looked about at the altered skyline of the farm. Seen from a man's height, this field was a level plain, but a definite declivity could be perceived by a boy lying on his back. A saucer, on whose rim were aligned all the taller structures of the farm. There, the barn from which he had come, and the old locust tree. There, the old silo. His eye slid past the new metal one, nosing the sky like rockets on a launching pad. Nor did it acknowledge the low humps of quonset huts. What it sought—though sought in vain, hence the vertigo of loss—was the house, that jumbled pile of white-frame boxes, some laid lengthwise, some stood on end, the crazy angles of separate pitched roofs varying in direction of the axis, marking the addition of each generation—a lifetime then, now no more than the brief span between one matriculating class and the next, time devalued like all else.

Even awash in nostalgia, Boone's memory could not transform that beast into a beauty, although at some time in its history, its owners must have had some such miracle in mind, employing in the effort every conceivable Queen Anne scallop, filigree and furbelow. In the end it stood there, architecturally ludicrous but a triumph of the dressmaker's art, like nothing so much as those heavy-fronted, rear-bustled garments of the day, overly trimmed with passementerie and braid and lace, and wearing on top—its own little roof like a conical cap—the crow's nest with its oval eye.

That was such a place from which a child plucked from the civic hearth and perched on high might witness the great and unspeakable, initiand to Eleusian Mysteries. Gone. Burned down. In its place the pregnant curve of Bucky Fuller's geodesic form. Boone strolled in that direction, considering how in silhouette, without the daytime detail of tetrahedron struts, it had an atavistic look, a temple built by worshipers of chthonic gods.

He had almost reached the door before he saw her, a pillar of darkness only semi-detached from the larger darkness behind her. Like the Dome itself, the details were obscured, but starlight edged the form with a faint Kirlian glow and made visible the whites of the eyes.

"Melissa?" Boone recalled a fact of life handed down from father to son: all cats are gray in the dark. "Is that you?" He answered her silence as if it had been a question. "Can't sleep. Just out for a walk. You too?"

She denied him speech but not her smile, then withdrew within the deeper shadows, a caryatid once more, framing another door, but whether stationed as a guard or performing some merely symbolic rite, he was not sure. He preferred the symbolic view.

Right down his alley, symbols. Raised a Unitarian, all sweet reason and high ethics but no show, he had always hankered for a painted lady to carry on his shoulder through carnival-lit streets or, at the very least, an annual feast preambled by bitter herbs with a door left open, a wine glass untouched, for a messiah who had a standing invitation but each year sent regrets. Boone could still find pity for that disadvantaged child whose church could have served as labor-union meeting hall or a capacious lecture room for a rigorous, hence undersubscribed, adult education course. He pitied his father too, who thought religion could be de-mythed like a sickhouse fumigated of its germs; who believed in God, if by God you meant a magnetic linchpin for a wobbling universe; who read the New Testament as a secondary source in studies of historicity; for whom a freeze-dried diet of good works was sufficient nourishment for the soul; whose counsel to his children, however great their distress, was to stand up straight and speak up clearly and say what you mean and mean what you say—to which end he improved their vocabulary, believing no doubt he was tending to their moral growth.

This Windigo now was a man—or saint or seer, prophet or teacher—after Boone's own heart, not missing a chance to mythicize and mystify. Take Melissa standing there. His father would say something like

"God knows what they've got stashed inside. Drugs? Explosives? Stolen goods? She's posted there to keep you out—no two ways about it."

No two ways about it. That was the trouble with his father's coolly rational mind, bent on discarding all ways but one. Yet as easy to say the guard was posted not to keep him out but to welcome someone in. Who else but Elath on his feast day? A week of feast days, on any one of which the advent might take place. Unheralded, without warning, like an Inspector-General, the savior might drop in. Meanwhile, keep unsullied a holy state of mind; indulge not in human intercourse. To smile apparently was allowed.

No human intercourse? A devilish impulse moved Boone forward. Skipping all word play, he clapped Melissa firmly by the upper arms and closed down hard. She neither shrank from nor opened to his touch. The smile held, but he had to tongue it apart. Civil disobedience, not outright rebellion, was her tack. The very passivity of her resistance fired his violence, yet with all the mouthing of passion, it was only flesh pressing hard on flesh, unrooted in any real desire. A faint flutter, more like pain. Semi-hard rubbery cock. He felt a ripple of disgust, as if a caress had brushed the hairs of his skin the wrong way. But what caress? Her arms hung limply by her side, disabled by his grip. He let go, expecting, hoping, begging her to make her escape. Instead she tilted forward, arms still hanging there, like a Chinese tumble doll designed to teeter on its base. Her head lolled on his shoulder, some idiot thing severed from her will. He felt her tonguing his cold sweat, like an animal at a salt lick. Then nibbling little love bites.

Irene once had such a doll, he suddenly remembered. "Struck, not falling" was the Chinese name. Thinking of a doll relieved him of his terror. He reared back awkwardly, a man trying to regain his balance from a clumsy stumble, an accidental collision in the dark. The apology he mumbled was suitably inane, but no more so than her mumbled "Don't tell, don't tell." Don't tell what, he wondered, don't tell whom? That barely breathed injunction was strangely amplified in his head.

"I'm no talebearer," he assured her. No tail-barer either, it would seem. All he wanted now was to escape from her recovered smile. "Everything's changed so since I was here as a kid," he was inspired to say, "I keep losing my way."

She must have assumed that the way he had lost was that to the barn, and pointed accordingly. In no mood to quibble, Boone took off in the indicated direction. Time to turn in, he was half-convinced, until he saw the light in the loft was still on, Jane still awake. He wanted no more encounters. Veering sharply, he adopted a brisk purposeful walk which wound down to an amble. A contemplative stride but a mind completely blank. Underfoot he felt rutted tracks. Only then did he know where he was going.

The locked gates seemed less formidable than he had thought. A reasonable protective device—Boone could see that now, calling to mind the snail-paced tractors he had passed along these country roads. Teenage drivers, all. Muscular yet well-larded, like prime grain-fed steers. Drawn at dusk to the general store like moths to the one light in town. Bored with bowling. Aslosh with beer. What more likely exploit for such a crew, on such a summer night, than to hassle the weirdos who had taken over old Sopher's farm? Imagining a convoy of semi-trucks headed out for a little fun, Boone felt comforted to know the fence was wired.

He had really come here for the view and that was unimpeded by the fence. All that corn. The cash crop. He sensed more than saw an oceanic tremor in the darkness across the way. Attuned to silence, he soon could hear a sighing, a soughing, like the creak of timbers of a ship at sea. He stared himself into such a trance he did not hear Jane come up behind him, was startled at her hand laid on his bare shoulder.

"Boone," she said softly. "Come back with me. I don't like being alone up there in the barn."

Boone put his arm around her, drew her to him. "Listen," he whispered. "Listen."

It might have been the wind. But there was no wind. An animal, then? A hundred little animals. A thousand little animals scurrying, skittering, scampering out there. "Listen," he urged her. "Hear that crackle?"

Terrifying crackle, like a distant forest fire, mounting in intensity, miles away as yet but closing in. "There's something out there!" she cried. "What is it?"

Listen, was all Boone would say. He put a finger against her lips, cautioning her to be quiet. For a moment there was nothing but the usual cozy hum of night. An animal after all, which their voices had frightened. But then it started up again, the creaking, stretching, rustling, crackling . . .

"You can hear it!" Boone crooned. "You can hear it growing!"

Jane looked into his face and saw pure rapture. An awe as mindless as the corn itself.

Chapter VII

Jane awoke to birdsong. Still a novice to early mornings, she lay motionless, depressed by a fine day and everything outside either singing or growing. She wished she knew the names of the birds. The name of the tall shade tree outside the barn. The name of the ubiquitous little weed that curled at its tip like a tendril of green hair. And out of the ground the Lord God formed every beast of the field and every fowl of the air; and brought them unto the man to see what he would call them . . . In the clarity of dawn, Jane saw the numen in the name. What's your handle? the cowboys asked. You can't take hold without the name. Boone, she murmured, like one crying out in sleep, but that gave her no dominion over this new world that lay about her. A sense of incompetence enfeebled her like a disease of the marrow; she lay with knees drawn up, self-embraced—a small animal's instinct to protect its vital parts.

When she mustered the strength to turn over, she saw that Boone was still asleep, asprawl in the royal position. In sleep a king, but waking, no such matter . . . That brought a smile, creased by the crook of her elbow. Sweet vengeance to use that sonnet tag against him who had forced it on her in the first place. In those salad days of love, or at least of new acquaintance, it had not seemed politic to reveal she hated being read to. Listen to this, he would say, ignoring the ostentatious finger with which she marked her place in the book she was reading (silently, as was intended, or why have books at all, why not stick with bards?), overriding her own preoccupation with an entirely different subject.

Overriding. She frowned down an inappropriate libidinous twinge at the memory of their last conjunction. At least for once he had made silent love (hate, she quickly amended, I hate you, Boone). His usual style was that of a granting agency, entitled to a periodic progress report: do you like this, do you like that, is it good? For him, fucking was not enough. He had this need for intercourse. Not that he had shown much need for either lately.

Boone twitched, gave a little jerk. A dream of falling? Royal, she supposed they called that supine sprawl, because it usurped so much territory. But left the face exposed. His looked sad, the accepting sadness of a child accustomed to abuse. She hardened her heart, preferring to believe the cockiness of his waking hours. The hand nearest her groped in the empty space between the disjoined beds, came to rest dangling, limp, abandoned. Served him right. She was determined to be pitiless, harboring the resentment with which she had awoken as if it were the mad money of a teen-age date. She would not forget he had dumped her from his lap. The disjoining was of his choice.

Wide-eyed, she watched the room slowly fill with light. The flatness of the land had led her to expect a dawn coming up like thunder, but from what she could see it spread like a stain. Still, the fact that this was sunrise, however etiolated a version, was a matter of some awe. The word itself shone in her imagination with all the glitter of an elaborate production, something like Easter services in the Hollywood Bowl. That came from early childhood days dark until noon, black-out curtains drawn over blinds, early-morning cartoons televised in late-night rooms, father tiptoeing out to what he called work, as she herself was to tiptoe off to school, Lois sleeping late because Little Missy never could.

Funny stories Lois told, at Daddy's urging: tell them, honey, about the Pincher. Jane, allowed to stay up late for parties, cut her critical teeth on those performances. There was this man hired by the Office . . . After that flat beginning, Daddy took over, explained that movie stars had hard hours, up at dawn, on the set by six a.m., a schedule Little Missy conformed to with the tantrums of a six-year-old. The man who drove her to the set, who—except when cameras were turning—was always by her side, was understood to be her bodyguard, a symbol of the Office's concern for so valuable a property. His real function, only Little Missy knew. Let her eyes close, or head begin to loll, the Pincher saw to it that she stayed awake. And no one but Little Missy was aware how it was done. Not a job for your ordinary lecher, Daddy always ended, it required an advanced degree. Much laughter—Daddy told it well.

Little Missy. Sour epithet employed by Boone. As if pinched herself, Jane jumped out of bed, more for the one-upping Boone than anything the horizon had to offer. Wouldn't you know, in disgust she addressed the west-facing windows (through which, according to Boone, hay was once pitched). She would have to go outside to catch the sun in its act. She considered and rejected so energetic a response. To run down rickety stairs still carpeted with gloom was more than any dawn deserved.

The clock told her it was pointless to go back to sleep, nor did she feel the need. Which did not keep her from eyeing the unconscious Boone with dog-in-the-manger churlishness. She plodded heavy-footed across the room. The closet of a bathroom, with its unfinished walls, had all the primitive charm of an outhouse brought indoors. She supposed she should be grateful there was plumbing of any sort: an overhead tank emptied by a pull on a chain and a worn enamel basin like that at a dentist's, just big enough to hold spit. She was satisfied she was making a great deal of noise—the torrential flush, the spluttering of rusty water from equally rusty tap, her own spluttering and rinsing as she brushed her teeth, then the yanking open and slamming shut of warped drawers in the old pine dresser—but still Boone slept. A flaccid collapse of flesh, of muscle without tone, like the body of some drunk you step over on the street, having made sure he is not dead.

Drunk? That would explain a lot. The disconnection of their beds. The other night, his mooning over a field of corn. There was certainly the wherewithal on this farm to ferment a ritual brew—no doubt reserved for the males of the tribe, that would not surprise her. But Boone drunk and not showing it? She not knowing it? Two drinks were all it took and it was goodbye Dr. Jeckyl, hello Mr. Hyde. Except Boone, perverse as always, did the trick in reverse, his Mr. Hyde by far the nicer guy. Not at all like Alan.

The memory of Alan drunk was an unwelcome intrusion. She shook herself: come on, face it, you never loved his sweetness, you savored it only when you thought of Boone, the way you like papaya only when accompanied with the sour pucker of a lime. It's not love betrayed that still turns your stomach, it's your pretense at love—as bad, admit it, as his pretense at sweetness.

As it turned out, she felt only mild surprise when he appeared that evening with a bottle of Scotch instead of his usual flowers. She had not seen him take a drink, not even wine. What a day, he was beat, he said and looked it. We'll just watch TV, she said, obeying a competitive urge to outdo him in sweetness. Also not averse to showing him she could be domestic. She sat him in the upholstered monstrosity Boone had salvaged from the street, his satiric comment on her caned Bentwoods ("museum" chairs, in his opinion, deserving of a ribbon drawn across the seat to protect both cane and sitter). The Monster—as she took to calling it—dominated her own furniture by virtue of its size and ugliness, a shaggy mammoth excavated intact from ice to rot away in her living room. And yet, even with Boone dismissed, she could not bear to throw it out. No one could sit in its capacious lap, secured on all sides by its barreled back, without a sigh of sybaritic pleasure, knowing at last the full dimension of the word "comfort."

Proof that the relationship was advancing to another plane, Alan watched the news while she made pretty sandwiches with what she had on hand, taking pains to garnish them aesthetically. Here was a man who appreciated all her trouble and said so pithily: hey, that's neat. Unlike Boone (invidious comparisons kept leaping to her mind) who claimed that radishes abloom like roses looked half-chewed and then spit out. Still, Alan drank more than he ate. It took half a bottle for his tongue to loosen, and then what foul stuff came out. What meanness. Presumably aimed at his ex-wife but in generic terms that embraced all members of that species known as cunts. She was stunned, without words, without feeling, like an animal pole-axed by a butcher. Filthy cunts | he railed at large.

It took Boone, still skulking in her head, to supply her with her lines. "Synecdoche," she said, in the controlled falsetto of a ventriloquist's dummy. That's right, Boone's whisper assured her, the part standing for the whole. But for him, she whispered back, directing Boone's attention to the lout in the chair, the hole is the whole. Boone appreciated that.

Alan glowered. "If there's one thing I hate, it's a woman with a mouth."

Metonomy, Boone prompted her, and she spat it out.

"You filthy fucking cunt," Alan roared back.

(Only later, after hanging up on his apologetic call, did she realize he took her cool rhetorical analysis for cursing in a foreign tongue. "You speak all those languages?"—an exclamation early in their acquaintance that she had mistaken for awed admiration until she heard the boast behind his modest claim to only one. I'm honest, above-board, the translation went, what you see is what you get, whereas she was suspect in her ability to voice and understand strange sounds, as if in shifting from one language to another her very substance was transmuted, like the witch in fairy tales: now a beautiful lady, now a crone, now a panther crouching for the kill, now a common crow).

But the violence in this man would not content itself with words. When he tried to rise from the sunken deeps of the chair, she knew real fear. That he had trouble getting up was evidence only of how drunk he was, but she preferred to think that the Monster's barreled back, always so protective in its hug, was protecting her even now, constricting around him, holding him down, giving her time to escape. Her last look was at the terrible change in his face: rage devouring the features, shrinking the eyes, thinning the mouth (how could she ever have thought it sweet?). Safe on the street, too embarrassed to call the police, she had waited by the corner newsstand until she saw him leave, returned to find a carnage of lamps and dishes and chairs. And amid all that splintered wood and broken glass, the Monster sat, dilapidated as ever, but still intact.

So much for Alan drunk. Now Boone drunk was a dear—a bumbling playful puppy, the kind that jumps on strangers and licks them all over. In vino veritas, Boone's father had observed the night before the wedding. Sobriety and youth were the great deceivers, in drunkenness and old age the truth was revealed. So his father playfully warned her, though in double jeopardy himself. Let us hope, she had giggled, somewhat in danger as well. She liked Boone drunk, a pity he didn't indulge more often. Mornings after were another story. It was remorse and terror, not simple thirst, that wrung Boone dry.

What did I do, what did I say? Did I make a fool of myself? What demons did he imagine would get loose?

You told your father you loved him.

Boone groaned, swore never to touch another drop. Sent a baleful look in her direction, swore off all family gatherings. As if it had been her idea to spend their wedding eve at his father's. The old man needed cheering up, he had pleaded. She had offered no objection. Better that than the bachelor's party he had earlier threatened, irked by her insistence on the traditional.

A good idea, she agreed, and improved it, making it a joint family affair. She taxied her father down from his hotel—her contribution to the party, nicely wrapped in Palm Beach worsted. And Irene was at the door to welcome them with silvery tinkle, having moved back when her mother died.

All those years of sublets were now explained, Boone had said, Irene was on the waiting list for just this vacancy. Jane wrote that off as another cheap shot at his sister, for Irene's stint as hostess ended at the door and she made none of those little proprietary gestures to announce that this was home. In fact, to her father, she seemed a half-materialized ghost, a special effect of sorts through which he tried to walk, bumping into her when he came out of the kitchen to greet them, a lean old man with apron tied around his middle, waving a wooden spoon like a baton; bumping into her again when with a bachelor's flurry, he brought out the chilled champagne. Glasses, glasses! Boone's father cried, thumb already on the cork. Boone sprinted to the sideboard, made it back in time to catch the flow, passed the drinks around. To the happy couple, Jane's father presumed to toast. Irene just stood there, smiling like a guest.

Another bottle and the voices of the men filled the room, arguing, but still friendly, about the Arabs and the Jews. Boone's father threatened to turn serious. Her father switched to ethnic jokes. Boone laughed at both. Jane grew weepy—where were the mothers? At least the late Mrs.

Everready had an excuse. Lois simply said no, she refused to be in the same room with Jane's father. (You have to understand, darling, it's nothing to do with you. Truer words never spoken.) Jane turned lachrymose and sought female comfort in Irene. But Irene was out of it. She had barely wet her lips on the toast, citing a distaste for bubbly stuff, had stuck all evening to tall clear drinks that looked as pure as Perrier but must have been half-gin.

"You had your bachelor's party after all," she accused Boone in the cab after they had dropped her father off.

Boone laughed. "It went pretty well, didn't it? My old man liked your father."

Which showed how drunk he was. Boone's father had hated her father. Thrown against her by a turn of the cab, Boone stayed there. Like a puppy, licking her all over. (She should have thought of Alan then, she would have valued more such sloppy loving.) Stop it, she said, and was appalled at the rage in her voice. The driver looked around. "Tomorrow," Boone said—and but for the bullet-proof glass would have licked him too—"tomorrow we're getting married."

The alarm went off. Unconcerned, she watched the clock, rocking on its back, skitter across the table, teeter on edge, crash to the floor, there to continue its shrill convulsions. She was already fully dressed, presenting to a shaken Boone an example of spotless virtue clad in slightly dirty jeans.

"What's going on?" he asked suspiciously, reaching down to throttle the alarm. "How come you're already up?"

No need to tell him she had slept poorly, in and out of dreams, manufacturing her own alarm. "I wanted to see the sunrise," she said, nicely circumventing truth. She was surprised that he, enthusiast of early rising, looked so groggy. "After all, it marks the high tide of my blood's flow." He gave no indication he recognized the jibing quote or that Melissa was its source. "How would you measure blood tides, by the way? With one of those rubber-cuff things? Or is that what you call an organic metaphor?"

This was role reversal with a vengeance—she spraying the air with words like some deodorant to wipe out bad smells, he saying nothing. She watched him dress, slowly coming back to life—he who usually sprang from sleep fully alert, moving from park to high gear with no intermediate shift, never stalling.

"Are you taking those antihistamines again?" she asked abruptly, reminded by his sluggishness that the medication had its side effects. That annoying habit of his—forefinger dug into ear, twirled like a drilling tool.

An itch was his complaint—well, hardly a complaint, an itch he'd had on and off for years, it didn't bother him at all. The complaint was hers: there he went again, reaming out the tunnel of his ear. The unspoken but deeper complaint: whenever she breathed love into him, he pumped it right back out. It took months of nagging to get him to a doctor—her doctor, Boone having none, assuming that with childhood shots he had graduated from patienthood. "Could be an allergy," he opines. "But then," Boone had derided, "what couldn't?" Still, the antihistamine had worked.

He hadn't used the stuff for weeks, he told her now. And the itch had not returned. Which proved her doctor was an asshole—and by association, she as well.

He was awake at last, as if it took a flow of bile to invigorate him. A fast shave and no time at all to slip into bibbed overalls. With uncustomary courtesy, he held open the door for her to pass through first—a courtesy, she noticed, that insured she kept her distance. Once outside, his grumpiness lifted like ground mist giving way to a fine morning. There was brisk eagerness in his step, an open cheerfulness in the face turned not to her but to the dining hall ahead.

Honeymoon. To Jane a word that suddenly dripped with gall. A week of marriage and already they were harboring a lifetime's worth of grudges.

They were now abreast of the dormitories, in time to be caught up in the orderly exodus. Casting a good-morning smile abroad, she looked for Rafe, caught sight of his golden head. Marriage was nothing more than a convenient travel arrangement—a timely remembrance. Her smile took aim, was received with a solemnity that promised more than any answering smile. *The real thing*, her whole body hummed.

Boone saw that exchange: Jane's radiant greeting, Rafe's solemn nod. He marveled at his own sang-froid, remembering with what chagrin he had initially reacted to Jane's erotic interest in the blond giant. Love, I love you, Jane, he had proclaimed and she had called it rape. He did not fail to notice that Rafe shared his coolness—not a crack of expression in that smooth face. He himself was now the object of Rafe's enigmatic regard. He looked quickly away, confused not so much by the probing stare as by the image that sprang into his mind: a lurid illustration in the World Book encyclopedia that he had pored over as a child. The Human Body. Full-page, full-color anatomical drawing with transparent overlays: turn the first and the skin peeled off, exposing the blood-red sinews of Man flayed alive.

The same queasiness struck Boone now as his glance flitted over the impassive faces of all these acolytes. Peel off the skin of gravity, reveal the raw musculature of smiles.

At breakfast queasiness was with him still. So much for psychic readings of other people's minds—the uneasiness was in his stomach, he must be coming down with something. He felt better after chewing the ritual corn. The stuff should be packaged as an over-the-counter nostrum, bring in millions. Lenrek—Nature's digestive. Boone chewed slowly, ruminating on an advertising campaign. So many ideas surfaced, hard to follow through on any one—enough to lean back and admire the word-shimmering sleekness of their form, their porpoise-playfulness.

Jane leaned across the table as she rose. "Did you hear that? There's to be a party tomorrow night—inside the Dome."

Engrossed in filming a TV commercial for Lenrek he hadn't heard but nodded, accepting the return of friendly relations. The women filed out first—an opportunity to survey the field. So far as looks went, on a scale of one to ten—he checked himself guiltily, as if Jane would read the thought, would turn back in the doorway, say: there you go again. Typically male, she would say. Typically male was her expression of deepest contempt. Women, she had informed him, don't do that kind of thing. He did not get very far by pointing out she seemed to have an eye for any man built like a linebacker. A woman is not blind, she emended slightly, but no woman measures masculine charms on such a mean competitive scale. Theirs, it would seem, was the kind of grading system Boone had no tolerance for—mealy-mouthed pass-fails.

He doubted he would give a pass to any of these faces except Melissa's; the lack of make-up must account for the absence of allure. And yet the movement of their bodies under the long shrouds of calico (he noticed with disapproval that Jane was back in jeans) was strangely like the shimmy of houris wrapped in veils, evoking an image of Moorish heaven where the maidens were all virgins, in whose ravishment lay an eternity of pleasure since they arose from each new fucking virgin still. Oh, God, we are mussulmen all, Boone groaned, feeling an equivocal pain in his groin—so shrill, so piercing, like the momentary vibration of a forgotten nerve, gone as quickly as it had come, he was not sure if it had been a response to his apocalyptic vision of male desire or mere urinary urgency.

The stab was to his memory too, some connection there with his father's scorn. A glorious everlasting fuck! Making the connection, he laughed aloud, causing the two men with whom he marched in step to look at him expectantly. "I just wondered if my father was familiar with the Koran," he said, leaving them with still-expectant smiles outside the Dome. Their job was to check the lighting inside for the morrow's gathering, his led him to the tractor shed. The assignment was to his liking, he would feel more the farmer astride that behemoth of a machine.

Parted from his companions, he no longer laughed. His father, once recalled, would not let him go, insisted that he relive the aftermath of his mother's funeral. To justify himself, Boone reworked his disgust at that whole show of bereavement. After all, his mother had died in bits and pieces, evicted from her many-mansioned soul room by room. She had paid little regard to the final demolition notice, nor did he, let Irene blubber all she would.

The only shock Boone felt was at the choice of service. He had expected burning, not a burial. Long ago his father had distributed two forms to the household with a clipped note: sign and return to me. Boone had read, signed, returned, thereby authorizing his cremation—no frills, please—and bequeathing to the needy all his organs like so many variety meats (still carried in his wallet the card advising whom it may concern of this prior lien on his body). Perhaps his mother had not signed. But how to explain the strict Lutheran service—an hour's worth of Lord Jesus Christ in chapel and an extra serving at the grave—if not by a sly recidivism on his mother's part? Not his father's, that was clear from the crotch-scratching and muttering at graveside: "Then said I, Lord, how long?" Boone hoped only he had heard that groan. His own pose of painful attention was meant to serve as reprimand, he was not really listening to the familiar drone of earth to earth, ashes to ashes, dust to dust, eternal life through our Lord Jesus Christ, so that when the next words sprang out at him, de-ritualized, with all the ferocity of the literal, he felt skewered through the heart . . . Who shall change our vile body, that it may be fashioned like unto His glorious body . . . Boone gritted his teeth, not to cry out: Even a progressive degenerative disease? Vile body. In the genetic sweepstakes, his mother had drawn exactly that. His tears—the first and last he was to shed—were more of fury than of grief.

As for that convivial aftermath of funeral meats, his father acting as bartender had poured such stiff drinks that all those distant cousins (lapsed Lutherans too, Boone could only assume) had dissolved more into hilarity than tears. Boone, knowing his weakness, had not touched a drop, his sobriety feeding his disgust. Found himself slobbered over by drunks who saw themselves as sinners, him as the saved. Like my short hair in college, he thought, feeling the same chagrin. Once again a constitutional frailty mistaken for an act of faith.

Through all that he had provided the proper filial support. And since his father no longer kept a car, had driven him to the monument yard to choose a stone. That is, had provided the car—his father had insisted on taking the wheel. I know the way, he offered as an excuse, as if he drove every day along that remote stretch of highway hysterical with flags of used-car lots. Another form to fill out: the epitaph. The charge made by letter count, his father turned laconic, put down just her name, her dates. Boone thought some sentiment should be added. In verse. Such as

> Now with our Lord Jesus Christ
> Who is a Whiz
> At changing such vile bodies
> Like unto His.

He had been good brother too, moving Irene back home. He did all the lugging while she stood on the brownstone stoop, warning him which cartons should be handled with more care. Even in that bitter cold, she kept her outerwear to hand-knitted shawls. Layering, she called it. With Cossack boots and ankle-length wool skirt, she had a turn-of-the-century look, right out of steerage. "Don't drop that one," she called out, hugging herself for warmth. "It's got my elephants." She collected elephants, only elephants with trunks upraised—a good-luck symbol. Unfortunately the trunks were always breaking off. He controlled his temper, even stayed to clear away the storage boxes cluttering her old room. His father hung about, carefully stepping out of the way; looking on, but never offering to lend a hand. You would think he was moving out, not Irene in. And after carrying all her stuff up the stairs, there were more boxes to be carried down. Leave those in the hall, Irene instructed, Goodwill would pick them up tomorrow.

"Glad to see you're getting rid of stuff," he had said with an obtuseness not to be remembered without a painful flush. "I've never known a house so full of junk."

"They're mother's things." Irene let that sink in. "Never mind, Boone, it's only right I should have that job."

My things. He heard his mother plain.

"There was a box—" he had to squeeze the words out through a bolus in his throat—"she kept it in the top drawer of her dresser. You didn't throw that out, by any chance?"

To hide whatever might show in his eyes, he glared at the cartons. Irene laughed: he looked like he was playing Superman again, using his x-ray vision. It would be easier if he just told her what kind of box.

"Red lacquer. One of those sleek shiny jobs. Like something in which a Japanese would pack his lunch."

Twelve, thirteen he must have been when he first looked at her and saw a middle-aged woman with a name other than mother. Mary Ashton Everready. Had she been pretty, Mary Ashton? It was a peculiar family, he knew by then, that kept no photographs. His father seemed to feel they were a mnemonic device for people of low intellect. "I keep it all right here," he'd say and tap his head. As for his mother, "There are some people who are simply born unphotogenic," she confessed, as to another congenital disease. Irene had told him that, before the days of plastic surgery, they shot aging movie stars through cameras screened with gauze; he tried for the same effect by looking through his lashes.

"Why are you squinting at me that way, Boone?"

"I was just wondering what you looked like before you married Dad."

Mock amazement in that exaggerated lift of brow. But she was pleased. He knew that from her eyes. The wry pursing of her mouth warned him she was about to say something sharp, her way of discounting any complimentary attention. "What you mean is"—but still she flushed—"you can't believe I was ever young." With a laugh—at him? at herself?—she opened the dresser drawer, burrowed in a lot of filmy stuff, pulled out the box. "Mind, you're not to ever touch my things," she warned.

A box of such high polish seemed fit repository for state secrets. Out came a passport, its mottled green showing travel wear at the edges. Slipping off the rubber band that held it to some envelopes with foreign stamps, she made ready to show him that her youth had been officially stamped and notarized. "Oh no!" she screeched and hid her face behind fingers spread like a fan, "I never looked like that!" Back snapped the band, back slid the passport, back went the box.

Of course the first time he found himself alone in the house he sneaked a look. Almost his nerve failed him—the crime not so much in laying hands on her private papers as in putting his gross touch on the snake-like tangle of her nylons, on the empty cups of her bras. His fingers left sweat marks on the lacquer; he had trouble lifting off the top. The envelopes banded to the passport were ancient, dated by the postmark, of a kind of flimsy paper he had never seen before. Addressed to Mary Ashton, not his mother. His mother, he corrected himself, before she was his mother. Love letters, they had to be—girls always kept them like hidden treasure. From his father, before his father was his father? Foreign stamps, but no return address; so his father was a traveler even then. He would have liked to know how such a man sounded when he spoke of love, but felt the full weight of that biblical injunction: no son should see his father naked. And if fear of God was not enough to stop him, fear of his mother was. Such thin paper was sure to crumble with the unfolding—a dead give-away. Still he took comfort in this evidence that they had loved each other—selfish comfort, sandwiching himself between their love, snuggling in it like a small child in his parents' bed. Nobly putting aside the letters, he opened the passport instead. Just as ancient, issued to a Mary Ashton too. Dry-throated, he drank in the forbidden view. A kind of terror squeezed his heart: the eyes of this young and pretty woman held no knowledge of his existence. She stared straight back and cut him dead.

"I know the box you mean," Irene said. "It had papers, personal stuff, I gave all that to Dad." She turned on him the forgiving look he so hated, its only purpose to make clear he had much to be forgiven for. "I had to go through everything, no one to help, I couldn't very well ask Dad, not in the state he's in. You know what I found hardest? Her underwear. What is there about underwear," she asked plaintively, "that's so painful when it belongs to someone dead?"

Boone was glad his was not the hand. *Don't touch my things*, he would have heard her cry.

He stood in the doorway watching his father pack his bag. A meticulous packer. As if every garment had a natural grain in accordance with which he made those precise folds with the edge of his palm. Even the knitted jockey shorts. Boone could feel the heat of anger like an alcoholic glow, even as he marveled at the smooth compression of a voluminous dark blue robe with satiny lapels—the kind never worn by any other mortal save Ronald Colman in movies of the thirties.

"So you've wangled another trip, I see. You haven't lost much time." The doorway in which he stood, the doorway to his parents' bedroom, was used to framing a more plangent cry. There he goes again, off to some god-forsaken spot, bringing back god-knows-what diseases. Even in her mobile days, his mother had not liked those survey trips abroad. She, for whom catastrophe was always hovering in the wings, was certain that it but awaited his father's departure to strike the plumbing, the children, or the car.

"I don't have much time." A half-moment of silence as absolute as zero. Was his father too about to die? "Next year they're retiring me, you know. After that—" he shrugged—"I dwindle into a part-time consultant."

Boone was unmoved. It was in the nature of fathers to dwindle. As a child he had watched his father pack as for an epic journey, seeing a Moses who crossed wildernesses to strike a rock with his staff: this is the site! And lo, Tower and Rowe would send out its minions to construct the dam, needless to say gargantuan in size (something like the Grand Coulee was what he had in mind)—one of those mighty sweeps of concrete that looked like Niagaras of water turned to stone, whose main function (as he now saw it) was neither flood control nor the generation of electricity but, like the Great Pyramids it rivaled, the advertisement of its builder's power. To discover that mini-hydros were his father's specialty, what a come-down. As for those epic journeyings, they were finagled by his father, much as a congressman contrives a junket, whenever he craved a respite from the drudgery of computerized design, a holiday from office politics. From wife and children, too?, his mother must have wondered.

Still, give the man credit—he had always returned. And it couldn't have been easy. Boone recalled his early dating years, how girls liked to break the ice with horror stories about their families. When his turn came, he found himself employing an engineer's vocabulary: tension, compression, stresses, trusses. Do you know how an arch works, he would ask, then quote his father quoting da Vinci: An arch consists of two weaknesses leaning one against the other to make a strength.

He wanted to be fair, even generous, but the familiar sense of holiday exuded by the packing still enraged him. He watched his father lock the case, secure it further by buckling its two broad straps. No flight-weight, easy-to-carry nylon for a man who still wore dressing gowns. The worn leather, kept buttery soft with constant saddle-soaping, announced to all the world that here was a man who, forced to give his custom to the airlines, in his heart still rode the trains.

"I'm glad to see that you are not exactly paralyzed with grief."

"Is that what you want—a paralytic on your hands?"

"All I want is that red lacquer box of mother's. Irene says she gave it to you." A puzzled look was all his father gave him in answer. "I don't see that it's so unreasonable to want something of hers to keep for myself."

"No, no, not at all. I was just trying to remember where I put it. Probably in the closet—yes, I'm sure, on the top shelf. See if it's there."

It was. Boone tucked it under his arm and stalked out. And stalked back in.

"There's nothing in it, damn you!"

"It's the box you meant, isn't it?" That dawn of understanding enacted in his father's face—pure pretense, Boone inwardly raged. "You don't mean you wanted those old love letters from before we were married? Had I known—I never thought—she was so private, I'm surprised she told you about them. Too bad, son, I threw them out, I'm afraid."

"There was a passport, with her picture. I suppose that's in the garbage too." Coldly he observed his father's grimace, a sudden crumpling of flesh like newsprint added to a fire just before it goes up in flame. Behold the poor widower in his grief? A sneer came easier than belief.

Boone remembered now to be surprised that there had ever been love letters between those two. "But I'm not surprised you junked them. You fought like cats and dogs, not what I would call a happy marriage. And then came all the doctor bills. You must be glad they're over, why pretend to mourn?"

"A happy marriage," his father repeated. His face had assumed its more familiar corrugated hardness. Like a storefront iron-shuttered after closing, his mother had been heard to mutter, preferring arguments to end in fire, not ice. Now, a man bemused, he allowed his head to bob thoughtfully. For a moment Boone mistook the ruminative gesture for his mother's nerve-damaged wobble, then almost laughed in relief. With laughter, as always, anger oozed away, a boil that had burst. In its stead, a tenderness, a warm flush of love coursing through his body like a transfusion of someone else's blood. Why are we always out of sync, he wondered sadly, not taken in by his father's smile, seeing below it the flat tautness of a cobra's head.

"A happy marriage!" Appreciative repetition, as if Boone had turned a particularly felicitous phrase. "How could I have missed that one? It should head the list!"

Boone eyed him cautiously, asked what list.

"Don't tell me you've forgotten. Poor little rich girl? Wise fool? Honest thief?"

Boone remembered. With his father, it was always word games. Like father, like son, he kept his own oxymoron list to which he was now being instructed to add happy marriage as the ultimate contradiction in terms. "Come on, dad, you don't mean that, any more than I mean what I just said about you and mother not being happy—"

"Happy, happy, happy." Sarcasm had always been his father's mode of child abuse. Hit me, Boone silently pleaded, as he had when a child, but his father never would. "Lately, I notice, happiness has taken on the aspect of a constitutional right. Guaranteed by the founding fathers. Life, liberty and the pursuit of. A bit weaselly, wouldn't you say, that wording. Typical of lawyers."

Boone waited. Was that all? His father folded and refolded a still damp towel as if that occupied all his thoughts. Boone edged toward the door, content to have offered a manly apology.

"Sit down, Boone. You've charged me with unhappiness—a cardinal sin. Allow me the courtesy of a defense."

Both chairs were occupied with piles of clothes. No place to sit but the bed. The long shelf above the headboard still demarcated his mother's from his father's side: hers the flat uneven stacks of paperback mysteries, green Penquins of the classic English school; his the upright hardbacks, thick-spined, mostly from university presses—a history buff's light reading. He chose his mother's side, hoping for less gore.

"You can use a short lecture on American history—what are you grinning at?"

Boone was adding "short lecture" to the oxymoron list. "Nothing, dad," he said, not without appreciation of his father's stance. What else but the full-hour lecturer's pose: one elbow resting on the highboy chest, fingers interlocked, a teepee formed with opposing thumbs. Like—the memory brought Boone perilously close to tears—his mother's game with baby hands: here is the church, here is the steeple . . .

"I'll keep in mind that you constructed models of the Nina, Pinta and Santa Maria in the third grade, thereby covering the subject to the satisfaction of the Board of Ed, but since you brought up that hallowed clause—"

Boone opened his mouth, closed it. Pointless denial.

"—let me ask you, do you not find it odd that those worthy squires, the original best-government-is-the-least-government crew, concerned themselves with a right—if you can call it that—so difficult to define and impossible to enforce? The pursuit of happiness!" Words his father rolled off his tongue as if mocking another idiocy of his son's coinage. "Now what do you think they meant by that? Since it's the one right you choose to exercise, I'm sure you've given some thought to what you're chasing."

Boone half rose, ready to admit to ignorance, to idiocy, anything, let him but leave the room.

"Before you commit yourself," the stern voice pressed him back, "let me remind you these were gentlemen of the Enlightenment, they knew their Latin, life required the sacrifice of private joys to civic virtue. As sensible men, their definition of happiness might strike you as overly modest. Something like—"

Into Boone's mind flashed a teeshirt with a Charlie Brown definition (or was it one of Snoopy's?) that he had treasured on his chest.

"—retirement in old age, a small estate somewhere in the country, no more public duties, time at last to observe nature and read Catullus."

Boone shook his head. Too long for a t-shirt.

"All right," his father said, as if accepting correction. "Some may have leaned toward the Benthamite persuasion—the greatest happiness of the greatest number—but were told to keep it down to twenty-five words or less. Needless to say, if you consult the courts, all they meant by that fine phrase was the right to get—and keep—your own. There you have it—man's highest aspirations reduced to t-shirt wisdom—" Boone raised startled eyes: had his father read his mind? —"Happiness is: the private ownership of property. I've often thought it was their one mistake, that particular passage. Maybe this nation's history would have been different, truer to their original intent, had they only written: life, liberty and the pursuit of meaningful work. Most men would find that happiness enough. But you—you—" fingers stood out in a tetany of controlled anger and Boone mouthed out come the people, taking childish comfort in finishing the rhyme—"you would never settle for something as ephemeral as that, what you want is a really solid achievement— a glorious everlasting fuck!"

Don't let a lion lick you, Irene had once warned him (unnecessarily, it seemed at the time), its tongue will take your skin off. So will Dad's, Boone had scoffed.

"As for your mother and me—"

"Forget it, forget I mentioned mother, forget the whole thing," Boone pleaded and fled.

"For your information—" his father shouted down the hall— "those letters weren't from me!"

Boone stopped, did not turn around, neck muscles tensed, shoulders hunched, as if the flesh knew better than he that the bombardment had not ceased.

"They're from her first love!" his father shouted, determined to be heard, however great the distance. "First and only love, need I say?"

Behind him, Boone heard a door slam. Down the stairs his feet led him into the kitchen. As if just home from school. As if his mother would be there, heating milk for his hot cocoa.

"You look like you could stand a pick-up," Irene said, hovering by the stove, waiting for the kettle to boil. "Sometimes it hits that way—as an aftershock," she said, placing before him a steaming cup.

He hardly heard her. Was vaguely aware there was something he should tell her. Or did she know already that the load-bearing element in this family structure was their father? He brushed his hand across his face, as if to cancel out all engineering terms, slow to realize the wetness was from tears. A man doesn't cry, his father had been taught, but had failed to pass the lesson on to him.

Inhaling the vapor of some strange herbal brew, he had thought: Here I am, in the house I grew up in, and I no longer know my way about.

Chapter VIII

Jane straightened up, massaged her aching back. "If it gets any hotter I'm going in."

No response. Melissa continued to pick tomatoes as if Jane had addressed that pointless threat not to her but to the heavens. Pointless, Jane was ready to admit—the heat was even more unbearable indoors—but at least it served to re-establish her volunteer status.

For much the same reason she had separated from the female contingent outside the dining hall, returned alone to her quarters after breakfast. An act of rebellion that warranted some notice, Jane had thought, half-expecting to be called upon by a committee, one with the ominous word "re-education" in its title. She stood watch at the window: a few free-ranging goats munched their way past the barn, but the Society sent no emissary, no one seemed concerned. The tinny but indestructible clock made quite a thing about time passing. With nothing to do, the only reading matter a Farmer's Almanac dating from Uncle Eban's time, she began to feel like a child playing hooky whose best friends were all in school.

The beds attracted her notice—their separation more than a matter of the few inches between. Boone's was made (how had he managed that so sneakily?), there was even evidence at the corners of an attempt at military precision. Skirting it, she patted the old sagging mattress for refusing to play along. Hers was a tangled mass of sheets with a declivity still boasting that here Jane slept. She lay spread-eagled, ready to sleep again but the day's heat was already drooping from the rafters and in the absence of human voices she became aware of a different kind of racket—a monotonic drone, like a great Ooom of meditation from the planet itself, varying only in intensity. Crescendo, diminuendo, crescendo. The insects' antiphonal response to Boone's corn. She moved heavy-limbed through dreams, awoke sweat-sodden, sought relief outside. Encountering Melissa with a large basket over each arm, she had asked meekly if she might come along.

"Why only the green ones?" was her new complaint. The stakes were breast-high, but she had been instructed to pick only tomatoes at the bottom, hard ones that did not show the slightest blush of ripening. This time Melissa answered, with no halt in wrist-work: the kitchen was preparing a special condiment for the Feast—it went very well with meat. Jane considered derisively the prophet Elath, who had decreed that ketchup must be green. His Feast couldn't come too soon for her. Seven days to put a meal on the table was a bit much.

A wind sprang up, making enough noise to convince Jane she was cooler. She moved along the vines, head turned away from what seemed fistfuls of sand thrown maliciously at her eyes. Now she was vying with Melissa, speeding up, determined to fill her basket first. The clear urgent cry of her name made her look up. Damn, she grunted, acknowledging defeat. Melissa at the far end of the staked row, basket on arm, was ready to go.

How silent it had grown. An enormous bated breath. There was still sunshine overhead, but dense black clouds had popped up in the west. A thick crayoning of black like the scrawl of an angry child intent on mutilating the blue text.

"We'd better get inside," Melissa called, waving her arm with the vigor of a swimmer's stroke as if to pull Jane along. To Jane the thunder sounded safely distant. More importantly, Melissa's basket was by no means full.

"Coming," she called back and Melissa trotted off—her usual pace, more or less—but no Jane panted after. Instead she inched her way along the row, filling her basket to the rim, then mounding it with more. She meant to leave no doubt that as a green tomato picker, she outclassed Melissa.

Darkness fell abruptly as a power failure. A flash of lightning, branched like the antlers of a stag, lit the sky with a neon glare. That's enough, Jane decided. Yet dallied to watch in awe as a real thunderbolt, hurled groundward by a Thor, struck the cornfields across the road. Like one of those nature photographs that wins third prize, she thought. But no photograph had prepared her for its premonitory hum, a kind of atmospheric tune-up, or for the acrid smell of ozone that was its aftermath. It occurred to her that in these flat fields she might well achieve her heart's desire, become at last the center of attraction. Run, don't walk, to the nearest exit. Run? She could barely totter with the over-weighted basket. In full panic she jettisoned the mounded overflow, tomatoes rolling everywhere like hard green billiard balls; then, shouldering the lightened load, raced for the nearest shelter. Which turned out to be the Dome. A momentary doubt—Private, Keep Out, This Means You emblazoned on her mind if not the door—was resolved by an explosive clap of thunder. The door responded to her push, she darted in.

Could one suffer vertigo looking *up?* Or was she disoriented by an architecture that melded walls and ceiling, mimicking the celestial curve outside. Halfway up the hemisphere, like a constricting ring, was a cantilevered mezzanine reached by twinned stairs that flanked the entrance in which she stood. In the shadowed recess beneath, a partitioning wall cut a secant across the circle—oh, the relief of a straight line, of space bitten off into private rooms with rectilinear doors.

Putting down her basket, she advanced with the shuffle of a gawker to the center of the Dome. On the whole, she decided, a bit like being inside an apple over-generously cored. The impressive hollowness was somewhat marred by the cat's cradle of looping wires that crisscrossed it, dangling a multitude of pointed light bulbs, Christmas-tree sized. Red, white, blue, yellow—like the ritual corn always on the table. How solemnly they ate it, and what a ridiculous noise they made cracking it in unison with their teeth—Boone the most ridiculous of all, slightly off in his masticating rhythm. Amidst such solemnity, the announcement at breakfast had taken her by surprise: *We will gather in the Dome tomorrow night.* A party, she had conveyed to Boone, though by no means sure such socializing was condoned by their faith. Whatever that was. But colored lights were an encouraging sign. So was the furniture clumped to one side—three long tables, a jumble of chairs. Furniture upstaged to clear the floor for dancing was a reasonable surmise.

In the gloom, she had almost missed another decorative attempt— art work of sorts. No, photographs, she made out, approaching closer. A portrait gallery, it would seem, unframed prints nailed at haphazard heights to raw two-by-fours, the underpinning for the mezzanine. All life-sized heads, all frontal views, all photographed in the brutal light preferred by passport agencies or the police. Faces of the middling young, evenly divided as to sex, a look of wide-eyed blindness, slack-jawed faith common to them all. This then must be the roster of the saved, Elath's own. She sought out Rafe. No Rafe. In fact, no face she recognized.

On closer look, the images showed a steep gradient in degree of aging—only a few sharp and clear, the features of most in varied stages of fading, acquiring in the process an historical vagueness, like prints, poorly preserved, pulled from an archive. It must take many years for such deterioration to take place, yet Boone had it from The Windigo himself that the Society dated only from the lease of Eban Sopher's land. No matter, she shrugged, still convinced that this array of heads had some connection with the taking of the Vow. All about her was the chill of religious intent. As if this were some sacred grotto where healing miracles occurred and these were pictures of beloveds, once crippled, once diseased, now permanently in health, affixed there by grateful kin as testament to our Lady's grace and the glory of the Lord. Or the prophet Elath, as the case might be.

But of course!, she almost cried aloud, remembering now the magic in her first Polaroid—the child watching in awe as a face appeared, features took form right before her eyes. And, instructions not followed, faded so quickly to something like these. She nodded knowingly at the worst of the lot, looking more like a corner of the cosmos than a human face, a vague oval of lightness in a dark Magellan cloud of hair: something had gone wrong with the development, some fixative required but not applied.

At that moment the lights went on. She looked up with an appreciative "ah!" What had been a mess of crisscrossed wires was now a jeweled web.

"Okay, they're on—" a voice behind her called out.

She whirled. The center doorway in the partitioning wall was open. There stood Rafe, staring at her as wide-eyed, slack-jawed as any of those nailed heads. The thought came in a wild cackle: we can't go on meeting like this!

"It's terrific," she said. Damned the dryness in her throat. Swallowed, tried for a lighter note. "Really festive. Like the opening of a new Chinese restaurant."

Not even a smile? Well, you can't have everything—she had learned that early enough in life. Boone laughed at her jokes but when had he looked at her like that? Devouring her with his eyes, was the only way to put it. Let's face it, she imagined asking for a divorce, your sense of humor never made me shiver with delight.

"I was just wondering about the pictures," she moved towards him since he seemed frozen in his tracks. "Who is the photographer? It's a one-man show, isn't it, there's no mistaking the style." Now came the smile, when she had given up being funny. "Did I say something foolish?"

He was about to confess the foolishness was his, to tell her he knew the real thing when it came along—all this she was sure of before he took a step, just from the forward hunch of his shoulders—when a hand reached out from the open door behind him, touched his arm, the unbandaged one. It was a magic trick—a touch and he disappeared. In his stead, The Windigo. No smile there. Her shiver now was fear.

"Surely you have been informed the Dome is closed to you. Why are you here?"

She pointed to the basket parked by the outer door, calling it as witness for the defense. "I was coming back from the garden when the storm broke. The lightning was pretty scary, I figured I'd better get inside, and quick. Besides," she added with somewhat shaky bravado, "why all the fuss? I've been invited to the party. So what if I came a little early?"

"You know the rules. The men have their work to do, the women theirs. During such times, we keep apart."

She forced herself to meet his eyes, all dark-brown pooling liquid contained by sharp-edged lids. Cow-like, Boone had called them. Juno-esque, Jane had the startling thought. The Windigo, she named him to herself, and her heart responded with the butterfly flutter of a missed beat. How conveniently "The," used as an honorific, bypassed all inflection of gender. That granite head, that gravelly voice could just as well be female at a certain hormone-diminished age. The fact that The Windigo alone was shirted took on a new significance. The looseness was evasive, the gathering strategic—a shirt designed for sexual ambiguity. Even so, there was a mild swell to the overall bib, not unlike the receding tide of now functionless breasts. She looked away lest he see the new awareness in her eyes; on second thought, looked back. What if it was nothing more than pectoral fat? Common enough in old men, as could be noted on any beach. Another miserly law of nature, she had once proposed to Boone—the conservation of breasts: whatever fatty tissue the female loses, the male will gain. Miserly is the bad word, Boone had defended nature, I call it thrifty myself.

True or not, the suspicion that she might be facing a member of her own sex restored her natural disputatiousness. "Men's work, women's work, as if work had a sex." She gave a jeering laugh. "Correction. In this place, work seems to be the only thing that has."

"We seek out the special competence in each, Mrs. Everready. That's why this farm now operates in the black."

A "ping" overhead, like the flick of a thumbnail testing crystal, a fizzle of wires burning, and the colored lights went out. In the gloom under the mezzanine, The Windigo turned into a pre-Columbian deity, squat and powerful, carved out of volcanic stone. No, Jane quickly rejected that image, where was the upright penis brandished like a battleaxe, or the gravid curves of breast and belly? Primitive deities left no doubt about their sex.

"Not much special competence back there," Jane took pleasure in pointing out. "I'm sure your women could do as good a job of wiring as that."

"I'm sure they could, with proper training. Just as we can grow corn with kernels of any size or shape, but only at the expense of its essential germ."

No question now as to his sex. He was a man, all right. And a woman was a woman was a woman. Or, as Humpty Dumpty put it with equal succinctness, when I use a word it means just what I choose it to mean. Jane wished fervently that Adele were here—the fervency a function of the safe distance between them, since she had yet to feel comfortable in the actual presence of the farouche woman her mother was now living with. To share expenses, that's important at our age, you know, Lois had explained the sale of her apartment and her removal to the upstate farm of a new friend. And expenses must certainly have declined, since Adele was a do-it-yourselfer with a vengeance

"It seems there is something else you wish to say?" The Windigo said in the receptive tone of a therapist—encouraging but not coercive.

"Oh, forget it," Jane said. No point in confronting him with Adele's construction skills. He would merely cast aspersions on her "essential germ."

So had Boone. Except Boone had put it more crudely: Adele was obviously a dyke. Jane winced at the memory of that visit to her mother, intended as no more than ceremonial. Her anger, she told herself at the time, was at Boone's use of such a homophobic term. "Will you tell me why you assume, after a mere handshake and a few brief words—"

"Brief, you said it, " he interjected. True enough, Adele had all but cut him dead, but that was shyness, hard to recognize in such an imposing presence.

"So any woman who doesn't take to you must be a lesbian?" (Beneath that cold question, a colder one addressed to herself: will you tell me why I brought Boone here, as if I had a real mother and we were going to have a real wedding?)

No answer to either question. She felt the levitating effect that comes from the release of indiscriminate rage. "I'll tell you why—you can't stand the idea that a mere woman could build this house practically with her own two hands—"

"And all post-and-beam construction, not one nail," Boone said, mimicking Lois's awed recital on the recently conducted house tour. "Just like her forefathers built—let's not forget those forefathers. Not that we could. They're all over the place."

That wasn't fair, the family portraits were discreetly hung upstairs. Downstairs it was all black-and-white stills of Little Missy and a collection of Coming Attraction posters relegated to the darker areas, marred as they were by the inclusion of Billy Drood. But recognizing the distraction, she kept to the point.

"If you mean there had to be men to lift those posts and beams, so what? Adele was the architect, the contractor. And that little greenhouse you step into from the kitchen—Lois says she put that in after all the men had left. She would have done the wiring too, Lois says, except for the insurance thing. You should see the workshop she has out back—"

"I know, your mother told me,." Again mimicking Lois's breathless admiration, "She has power tools and everything."

"Ha! That's it, isn't it? Power tools! I see."

An *I see* so laden with significance, so colored with contempt, it drove Boone from the room. A slam of the door. *I see, I see* echoed through the emptiness he left. She threw herself on the bed, squashing a pillow over her head, as if still trying to blot out the image of Little Missy on Boone's TV. This was not the time to admit how much she herself disliked Adele.

What do you see in that woman? Not a question at all, Jane had realized even at the time of asking. Rather a statement of disapproval telephoned to Lois after her first visit upstate. She did not care for a woman who subjected every acquaintance Jane mentioned to ethnic scrutiny ("What kind of a name is that?"), who named her cats, all ten of them, after Republican presidents, who believed fanatically in animal rights (a loaded shotgun always at hand for trespassing hunters) but had little interest in human ones (sterilization, she had suggested, was the best answer for welfare mothers). And, not least of her crimes, had shown disdain for translation as a profession. (Her definition of a polyglot—this she offered with a wink at Lois—was someone who had nothing to say but insisted on saying it in as many different ways as possible. "Oh, I must remember that," Lois had applauded.

"What a question" was all Lois had for an answer. "I'm sorry you don't like her, she likes you."

Jane gave a short incredulous hah! She did not believe for a moment in those jerky outbursts of affection, mainly produced at her arrival and departure. They were put on, she was sure, for Lois's benefit.

"She *does*. She's just undemonstrative. It's that old New England stock, you know." And Jane had to listen again to how old that stock was, wondering if *that* was the attraction.

I see, I see. She was staring at the Windigo but what she saw was a terrifying view, the insides of her own mother. A quivering pulp of powerlessness. Exactly like that inside the child Jane, brain-washed by the prowess of the fabulous moppet on the screen, who not only could save a plantation or an army or a group of frock-coated, stomach-proud men called a political party, who not only could succor the needy and wheedle the wealthy, but who—this the child Jane had painfully noted, still of an age to suffer the occasional mishap—never had to pee! What she saw now was that the child Lois must have been just as intimidated by that blown-up black-and-white image, not quite knowing what was make-believe and what was real, or worse, knowing the difference only too well: Lois was make-believe, but Little Missy—*she* was real.

Seeing that, she could see what the grown-up Lois had sought for in that sad array of men she had lived with after the divorce—an ability to control events, to cope with crises, that sheer competence in living so lacking in herself when compared with the role she had played. Men who had turned out to be as foolish, as feckless as Billy Drood, with not even his comic genius to soften her scorn.

But not Adele. If Boone was right and they were lovers (at their age? Jane gave a disgusted shudder), then what Lois loved was those power tools. And Adele? Who had all but papered her house downstairs with Little Missy stills? She was in love with a superannuated child star.

The Windigo sharply called her to order. "We have our work to do in the kitchen. You will find it safe to go now." His gesture—a sharp sideward cut through the air, hand extended, palm down—put finis to the storm.

But not to me, Jane swore, even as she moved to retrieve her basket, it won't be long before we kick you out. Having framed a properly mocking goodbye—"*Oh, well,*" she would sniff, "*I guess I know when I'm not wanted*"—she turned back to discover there was no audience for its delivery. The door was closed. In a flash of rage—how she hated doors shut against her—she considered marching into the back room, telling him, telling the whole damned male crew exactly what she thought of their Society. Or better yet, defacing this cold empty kiva with a subway vandal's arrogant scrawl, nothing arty, just her name and the number of her street. Yes, defacing was the right word for all those heads like mounted trophies on a wall—so she saw them now, not as religious testimonials but as victims of a hunt, like those decapitated antlered deer whose eyes (glass, she would tell herself, just glass) had always moved her by their sweet pacific gaze, their utter lack of comprehension of their own death.

The weight on her arm reminded her she was holding a different kind of weapon. For a moment she relished the thought of a basket filled with red ripe tomatoes, envisaged their bloody splatter adding a proper martyred look to the surround of beatitude. Too bad these were so hard and green. Regretfully she turned to go, turned back, stuck her tongue out at one and all. Blinking in the bright sunlight, she marveled that the sky showed no vestige of the storm and that, after so childish an exit, her good humor was equally restored

Chapter IX

Much to Boone's chagrin, the lesson of the day did not involve the tractor. First things first, everything in its season, Marco said, cheerily sententious in his role of tutor, and led the way to a self-propelled machine with roofed cab for the driver. "It won't be long before we have to get the corn in, so you'd better learn how to operate the harvester."

A real antique, Marco apologized, misreading the disappointment in Boone's face. Unimpressed Boone remained even as Marco displayed its well-oiled inner workings—the rollers, chains, gears, the elevator by which the finished product, snapped and shucked and shelled, moved up the tall metal throat as if by peristalsis. As yet unattached, the trailing hopper, Boone hardly needed to be told, would catch the vomit.

A long-necked, plant-eating brontosaurus—Boone dismissed it with contempt. Like every kid, he had preferred the tyrannosaurus rex. Boone's gaze passed on to a neighboring appendage. He pictured himself riding high in the open, drawing behind that array of knife-edged wheels. It would be like driving a monstrous version of Messala's chariot, he thought with relish. A rotary hoe, Marco said, approving his pupil's keen interest but not his timing.

Everything in its season—Boone knew the catechism. Now was the time for confinement in a machine that made the rattling clanking noise of an ancient factory going at full steam, requiring Marco to yell instructions. It took most of the morning to learn to steer with the necessary precision not to break down extra rows, to engage and disengage the snapping rollers, to grow accustomed to the clutches, both foot and hand. And when dismounted, all those safety rules to bear in mind. Apparently the picker, unable to distinguish in its chewing between the operator and the corn, was not so strictly vegetarian as he had assumed.

A sudden ambuscade of black clouds made Marco call a halt, suggest they break for lunch. Gulping down a sandwich in the open doorway of the shed, Boone watched the thunderstorm pass by—all rhodomontade, not a drop of rain. Marco and the machine-shop crew, perched on a workbench in the rear, made quick work of the noonday meal, with much verbal smacking over the Feast to come. Boone wondered that the prophet Elath had not come up with something new—must all religious rituals boil down to food? Was this the sum total of man's spiritual advance: what once he offered to the gods, he now devoured himself?

They were in high good humor, much joking in the male mode, fondly insulting. An anomaly, though—all men together and not one joke about sex. Boone, even when the point escaped him, joined the union of laughter, found it restful that women were absent, even as butts.

A mistake—he knew as soon as he made it—to note their absence. Try *not* thinking of a woman now. Like that other game invented by his father (or so he was led to believe): try not thinking of a white bear. The time, five minutes; the stake, a whole dollar. Years later, encountering in Tolstoy the same challenge, he had exploded into laughter, not so much at his father's plagiarism as at the memory of Irene, face screwed up like a prune, attempting by sheer muscular contraction to shut out a white bear.

Again Irene, equally obtrusive. *You never think of Irene*—that from Jane, her self-appointed ombudsman. I do my best, he had acknow-ledged modestly, having just come from a very taxing dinner with Irene. Irene on a new high—Selfishness. "Oh, Boone, Ayn Rand is a truly great thinker." That breathy voice, by which he knew she had had enough to drink, made even her order to the waiter—"I'll have the free-range chicken"—sound like a mating call. The waiter leaned over her with the brio of a dark Latin about to sweep her up into a tango. She looked up at him with the smile of a cinquecento Virgin relishing her Assumption. While they discussed the choice of vegetable, Boone struggled to recall what great thoughts could be attributed to Ayn Rand. In his own cursory reading, he had found nothing more than the evaporated salts of Adam Smith, nobler elements steamed away. Nasty tasting stuff.

Irene's hand on his wrist called a halt to his slow loving spread of butter on bread. "You won't have to worry about me any more, I have learned the secret of true inner peace. After all this time."

She shook out her napkin, signaling that not another word would pass her lips. A pro forma closure.

"So what's the secret?" he consented to ask. She had chosen a secluded table for two, candle-lit. Boone cursed the darkness, reduced to feeling out his food.

"It's so obvious once you see it, you've probably known it all along." A diffident admission, strained through half-chewed chunks of chicken, trailing brown sauce down her chin. Anorexia had never been her problem. Be thankful for small favors, Boone could hear his mother say, small favors being all that God was handing out. Irene leaned forward. He smelled singed hair. Oh, oh, here it comes, he thought, and moved the candle. "I am *not* my brother's keeper!" she whispered, as befitting a secret.

Somewhere on that long boring stretch of Midwest highway, nothing but soybeans, porkers and salvation on the radio, he had thought to entertain his bride with a report on Irene's latest conversion.

"Selfishness?" Jane's high-pitched incredulousness annoyed him. "Your sister doesn't have a selfish bone in her body."

"How can you tell when she's so well-padded?"

"You know I hate that kind of crack," Jane said coldly and Boone had turned the preacher back on. Goddamit, he had a right to be annoyed. The economy of siblings was zero-sum: saying Irene wasn't selfish was as good as saying that he was. The sandwich had gone down too fast, Boone diagnosed the pressure on his chest. Unless it was Irene sitting on it.

She had done that often enough, he admitted wryly, during those growing years. Right here on the farm, in front of the house that was now a Dome, she had wrestled him to a fall. Uncle Eban stood on the porch, laughing his head off. Aunt Flo, a grey shadow behind the screen, materialized into harder substance when she flung open the door. *Shame on you, shame on you*, she had hissed, shaking Irene. *Sitting on top of a boy like that.*

"See you later, I'm going to walk it off," he called back to the still boisterous crew, rub of stomach pantomiming gastric distress.

"Better get in training," was the last he heard, "there's heavier eating yet to come."

Irene accompanied him on his amble. She would like it here—a new religious sect tuned in to heavy eating. And remember that old house you hated, he would write her, you'll be glad to hear that it burned down.

"You're going *there*? On *your honeymoon*?" Her look of horror made him laugh—a boy's glee. She used to look like that when he had dropped a bug down her front. Immediately he felt guilty—she had a knack for making him feel in the wrong. It was his inheritance, he said loftily, he was not about to sell it, and aha, came the thought: she's really sore because Uncle Eban didn't leave the farm to her. My just desserts, he almost told her, for that one summer I was forced to visit—remembered just in time that she had been there too. A remembering that never quite took hold. But if he kept forgetting, wasn't that what she wanted? She never spoke about it, it was as if she had never gone.

"How was your summer?" was the first thing they were asked after their father had pronounced them fit as a fiddle, judging—had to be assumed—from their wholesome scabs and scratches. Irene said nothing. It was left to him to provide a noncommittal shrug.

His father asked more forcefully, "Did you have fun?"

They were eating take-home pizza. After so long an abstinence, ambrosial was the smell and taste. "No," he had said. His father's raised brow demanded some elaboration, so he had added, "There weren't any other kids around; they didn't even have TV."

It was high time he learned to manufacture his own entertainment, his father said, and his mother nodded yes, yes, yes. He had never thought before of fun as a skill to be learned, like tying shoelaces. Stretching out, then tonguing up the rubbery strings of cheese, he had wondered if he should tell his parents the kind of entertainment people manufactured when they didn't have TV.

"And did you learn to milk a cow?" his mother asked. The way she leaned forward, both hands spread to cup her pointed chin, lent great importance to the question, although he knew it was just to stop the shaking. No, he hadn't: shame-faced admission to a failing grade. He had gone into the cowshed only once, hadn't liked the smell.

His father laughed. "I don't remember much of my one summer on that farm, but I do remember that—they made me clean it out."

No reason to admit that Uncle Eban had tried to make him do the same, but he had hidden until they gave up looking, gave up calling. Either the crow's nest was forgotten or it wasn't worth the climb.

"I learned how to kill a chicken," he offered to his mother, who had shown her disappointment that he hadn't learned to milk a cow. He felt resentful when she made a face. It was a learning experience, he would have thought.

His father took it more in stride. "Okay, so you learned to kill a chicken, hot stuff. Now, Irene, let's hear from you, what did you learn?" Irene said nothing. "What's the matter, cat got your tongue?" And yet, when it came to going back the next summer, what a temper tantrum she had thrown.

I won't go, I won't go! He felt a jolt as if his foot had misjudged the level of the ground. A boy's bellow, not Irene's. Like a fuzzy sound track that suddenly had cleared, the words rang in his head as if just shouted, and the tendons of his neck were as taut, his throat as raw as if the scream had just emerged. Then where was she—erstwhile kicker, biter, screamer—in all that brouhaha? He sees her now as encased in a glass booth of silence. His mother shakes her head—movement without tremor, deliberate with disapproval. His father turns to his favorite.

"What say, girl? It seems your brother has not reached the age for rational discussion. Wouldn't you like to spend another summer on the farm?"

The boy wonders what could be more rational than "I won't go!"

"If Boone doesn't want to go, it's all right with me."

That must have marked her exit. At least his father spoke of her as one no longer there. "It's all right with her," he mocked, "suddenly everything's all right with her. For God's sake, where's her spunk? And I used to think she was the one who would amount to—" Abruptly he switched tracks the way parents do when they see a child is listening. "As for you, young squirt, you'd do well to acquire a little of your sister's self-control."

With the headshake of a diver coming up for air, Boone looked about him. His aimless walk had brought him smack against the Dome. Had he wanted to obliterate all memory of the original house, he would have designed just such a structure—a simple hemisphere stuck like a leeching cup to the bosom of the earth. Reaching above his head, he touched a parchment panel, found it toughly resilient, with a slight waxy feel. Against hailstorms and high winds, what better choice than animal skin? Goat, it must be assumed (though skin shaved, scraped, defatted, stretched and smoothed and softened is more generic than specific), salvaged from the seven-day indulgence in meat granted by the Prophet Elath on the occasion of his feast. A highly movable feast. If there was some rhythm to its occurrence, Boone had yet to discover it in the reminiscences he had heard.

A low rumble of voices alerted him to the presence of men inside. In one of the troughs of silence between waves of talk, Rafe's voice rang out distinctly. Boone thought better of joining them. After all, he had been assigned to a different crew. But at a safe distance from the object of his dislike, he no longer heard the call of duty. He had had enough of farm machinery. Instead he felt an urge to view again the green dynamo across the road, whose energy set his blood a-tingle. Or could it be the charged fence, to which he had stood so close?

Passing the kitchen, he had a glimpse of Jane perched on a stool, looking as glum as the class dummy when *McGuffey's* was the reader and such punishment the rule. Another sign of how she held herself aloof from the group, for in a kitchen of her own she rather liked to cook. He scuttled by—if he were seen, she might come out and claim him. Just as he feared. In spite of his precautions (darting past the door, ducking beneath the windows), in spite of her blindness to his passage (she had not turned her head, nor raised up from the stool), she had claimed him. By, of all things, her cooking.

Sporadic, uneven, scorning the every-day, heavily into the exotic and adventurous—so he remembered now Jane's cooking. Always by the book, it seemed, requiring metric cups, clusters of gradated spoons, Pyrex bowls quantified by red scorings—instruments of laboratory precision. And how scientifically she measured, even leveling off the spoon or cup with a knife. "One and one-quarter, okay," he could hear her say with that little smack of satisfaction, a job well done. And then—his throat clogged up, the memory was so endearing—she would stand back, frown at the bowl, frown at the book, and surreptitiously fling in an unquantified amount, muttering, "Just a smidgeon more, I think," before proceeding to the next exact measurement, which in turn would be corrected by her intuitive sense that something more was needed—a dollop, a pinch, a lump. He loved her for that. The full generous measure. Under his eyelids, a strange prickle: why was she not that generous to him? A smidgeon more, Jane, he wanted to cry—not this love measured by the spoonful, leveled with a knife.

"I am glad to see you here," said The Windigo, immediately behind him. Boone jumped. "I just thought I'd take another look at the corn." Hearing himself all but stammer—like a kid caught wandering in the schoolyard when he should have been in class—he flushed with anger. He had every right; abruptly his pugnacious stance gave way, he felt disjointed, teetering off balance. It was the "real corn" (so he still dubbed it) he had started out to see, so what was he doing here at the experimental seed plot?

The Windigo's nod was approving. "The eye of the Master fattens the corn."

Like a boxer rebounding from the ropes, Boone came out jabbing. "I thought it was fertilizer that did that. I couldn't help but notice you've got a spreader back there."

Only for the cash crop, The Windigo said dismissively. Opening the gate, he stood aside to give Boone precedence. Determined to go his own way, Boone struggled to render his refusal just as politely. Or should he firmly state that cash to him was no mean epithet, he preferred to fatten with his eye the crop across the road? The Windigo was waiting, the sheen of sweat adding polish to the grandeur of that head. Boone stared, tongue-tied, at the broad pyramidal nose, the heavy planes of cheek and forehead, chin and jaw, giving the sense of something harder than bone, denser than flesh. Without a word, Boone passed through and The Windigo relatched the gate.

"Here we use only the compost from our pile and here no machine is required to harvest it." Boone winced, recalling his recent poor performance on the harvester. The twist of thick lips that passed for a smile—

underachievers must be encouraged—merely added to Boone's resentment. "We must go back to the beginning," The Windigo continued, "when man tended corn with his hands, fed it with his thoughts, shared with it one soul."

Ah, Zen and the art of farming. Enough of that, Boone decided, noticing where they were headed. No more good dog, keeping to heel. "That shed is too damn hot for me, I think I'll call it a day. See you at dinner."

The Windigo placed his hand beneath Boone's elbow as if helping him up a curb. "We've got the generator working again—don't you hear it? You are more likely to find it uncomfortably chilly. However, we shall not stay long. I speak of the beginning, but all this"—with his other hand The Windigo waved at the seed plot—"is but a first small step in that direction. You must see how far we have yet to go."

His plea, "too hot," being only an excuse, Boone was all the more piqued to have it thus countered. There was something to be said for childish tantrums, simply shouting "*I won't go!*" Being grown up, he could only whine that he was really beat, couldn't they do this another time?, even as he stepped inside.

The sticky heat was immediately replaced by a clammy cold. And what a noise, the generator's throb turning metal walls into a tuning fork. It was like being inside a sick headache, Boone thought, and continued his whine. "Let's make this short."

"Here we are." The Windigo pulled out a tray, stepped aside to afford Boone a better view. Like the generator's throb, some powerful emotion hummed beneath the man's grave composure.

"What the hell is that?" Boone asked, his own excitement detumescing in a harsh caw of laughter.

The Windigo reached in. Broad, squared-off hand, thick spatulate fingers—like a primitive instrument for tilling the earth. With an effort, Boone focused on what the hand was holding: a rusty-black, rough-surfaced object, no bigger than the first joint of the dark thumb. An old arrow head, a flint tool? Uncle Eban had spoken of nearby Indian mounds. But the shape was cylindrical. Besides, too small. A fossil then? A trilobite would be about that size. Infected with the collectomania of the teens, Boone had been fossil-hunter for a while. He looked closer for washboard markings, could make nothing of that shaggy surface. More like the scales of a miniature cone, dropped from a bonzai pine. Whatever it was, the proper response—if he took his cue from The Windigo—was awe.

"I thought we came in to look at corn," Boone said with a disinterest somewhat false.

"So we did. And so this is. Corn as it was five thousand, six thousand years ago. Before its cross with teosinte—see how each kernel has its own husk?"

All Boone could see was the puny head, flower-spent, of some grass-like weed. "It doesn't look very edible," he said, grinning at the picture of it being served buttered on the cob.

But of course it was edible, he was told sharply. These specimens had come from a cooking hearth in the mouth of a cave, an excavation millenia-deep. He was urged to look again—a backward student who had missed the point. Boone looked again at kitchen garbage five thousand years old.

"And this is what you hope to breed back to." This shriveled dwarf. This monstrous fancy, this misshapen dream.

"Let us say this is the avatar toward which our thoughts are bent, our hands are guided." The Windigo had the transported look of a believer in converse with his god.

Boone shuddered. The refrigerated air seemed to be condensing on his bare back. "It's too damn cold in here for me," he said and broke his way out into the sunlight where green things were growing that, however maimed and misbegotten, he could recognize as corn.

"Oh good, here she is," Melissa announced Jane's arrival, "I told you she was just waiting out the storm."

The four women in the kitchen looked approvingly at Jane's harvest. That was Donna, tall and thin—willowy? No, cadaverous Jane put it bluntly—who swept the basket into her embrace, murmured "Lovely, lovely," as to a floral offering. Thin cooks did not inspire confidence in Jane, and here was one who did not have the tact to conceal the sinuses and sockets of her skull, whose wrists were little more than bracelets of bone. From her perch on a high stool, Jane watched with proprietary concern the careful rinsing, the swift chopping of the product of her labor, her attention shifting from the macerated fruit to the twists and turns of Donna's knobby wrists, their juggler's skill, the graceful sweep of the long attenuated hands. That thinness, which had first repulsed her as a denial of the appetites, now entranced her with intimations of distilled desire, as if all the sweetness normally in flesh were concentrated in the marrow of the bones.

Forgotten in her corner, she observed the other women as they went about their chores: Melissa fondly pinching pastry rims in a row of tarts; the short and chubby one, russet-colored both in eyes and hair, scrubbing down a wooden cupboard; the meager blonde, elbow deep in a laundry tub, tossing a wash of salad greens. Ordinary movements, but choreographed to some music whose vibrations she could sense but could not hear. Jane suspected them all of humming under their breath.

Ordinary faces too, but with an almost pre-pubertal sleekness. No lines, Jane marveled, and recalled for the first time in years her best friend in tenth grade. Amy Pearsall, professional beauty at fifteen, with no time for study, no use for boys. Who, for reasons never fathomed, chose the captain of the girls' softball team, barely fourteen, as repository for her secret lore (or so Jane considered the make-up tips, arcane wisdom to be preserved for the world should Amy pass on, as indeed she did, moving to another city before the end of term). Jane was advised how eye shadow could increase the too-narrow span between her eyes, how blush could hollow out the plebian fullness of her cheeks, how lip color (always a brush, never a stick) could refine her too-gross mouth. Don't hunch so, don't slump so, take up tennis, drop softball, but what to do about that bottom? Never mind, thank God for plastic surgeons.

Jane thanked God instead that Amy wasn't into diets, her thing was lines. Let her hear Jane's raucous laugh ricocheting down the hall, let her catch Jane frowning over a tough exam, she would take her protégé into the tactful privacy of the john and, standing by her side before the mirror, use her fingernail, a perfect oval (they came in packets, she glued them on) to scratch red streaks between Jane's brows, around her eyes, furrowing deep the faint declivity from nose to mouth. A preview of a horror show: Jane's face at thirty. Jane understood. To be beautiful required that she never find anything funny or tackle anything hard. A hopeless project. Amy disappeared, leaving behind a thick-lipped, lumpy-cheeked, hunch-backed girl with meanly close-set eyes.

It had taken ten years, and half as many lovers, before the mirror reflected an approximation of what others saw. And now, in the bustle of this kitchen, it was all falling away, the easy cohabitation of her self and body. In its place, that old familiar squirming, the painful embarrassment of the ugly and ill-formed. In revenge, Jane trained on them Amy Pearsall's eyes: not a beauty in the lot (Melissa might have made it, but for that heavy jaw). And still she felt an inferior breed, just as she had in those make-up sessions long ago. So would I look like that if I took the Vow? It was a question someone else might have asked, so spontaneously had it risen to her mind. In a flash Jane recognized the look they had in common. It was pure happiness that made of them a race apart.

"I think I'll go back to the barn and lie down—the heat is getting to me," she said, suddenly anxious to leave the room. She found it difficult to unhook her legs from the cross-struts of the stool, a clumsiness that she thought must lend credence to her complaint, but beyond a perfunctory cluck from Melissa, there was no sign they cared. "I'm not much good in a kitchen anyway," she lied. "Of course, on your feast day I'll be glad to lend a hand—there must be lots of carrying to do if we're eating in the Dome."

"Oh, not so much," Donna said, but did not look up from the cauldron she was stirring. "The Dome has a special kitchen, just for Feast day cooking. Except something like this—" she tasted the green sludge, gave a satisfied smack—"must really be made in advance."

"Don't you worry about the feast—your presence is all that's required." At least Melissa looked at her. Jane returned her smile, but feebly, as befitting one with heatstroke, and left the happy crew.

The aborted storm had left the air palpable with heat, to be pushed through with sweaty effort. In a matter of minutes, her shirt was plastered to her back and she could feel beads of dirt in the creases of her neck, but better out here than in that kitchen steamy with content. Happiness was something she was never at ease with. When it struck her—a sudden reversal in her emotional climate, like one of those flip-flops in the earth's magnetic poles—she felt the giddiness of a new smoker with no tolerance for the vice. Struck was not the word—she and happiness did not collide, rather it brushed her like a comet's tail and she sailed through it, in and out of it, aware of nothing but a freaky change in weather.

Though she had headed for the barn, as announced, she had had enough of lying on an unmade bed in attic heat, veered instead toward the patch of shade provided by the locust tree. Here, on ground hard and knobby with exposed roots, she stretched out her legs, leaned back against the rough trunk and, with no one to intrude upon her but an otherwise occupied file of ants, slipped into the comfortable fit of sadness. Let Boone be seduced by all the promises that shimmered in the air: you too can be at peace with yourself, at one with the universe (circumvallated with electric charges), you too can be happy, can be whole. She preferred her old bits and pieces, thank you, this easy habit of discontent. Perhaps happiness was a language with its own complicated grammar and syntax, whose learning was controlled by a biological clock much as man's spoken tongues. Either you learned it at your mother's knee or were doomed forever, like the Wild Boy of Aveyron, to an emotional ferality, to grunts and snarls and groans.

At Lois's knee? Fat chance, she muttered and picked up a fallen twig to damn the flow of ants, grumpily watched the resulting traffic jam, the line reconstitute itself in a detour. Even in that reedy-columned Colonial of her parents' brief cohabitation, there had been no sign "Happiness Spoken Here." Passion, yes, behind closed doors, only the tearing and rending on public view. And then Lois's pitiful post-divorce performance, a regular Little Missy soft-shoe routine, dancing in and out of this career and that—real estate, bookshop, art gallery, Far East imports—appearing in each new production on the arm of a different male partner. It didn't work out, Lois would say. The man or the business, it was never quite clear.

That moment of understanding in the Dome, the pity and the terror of it, could not stand against the surge of old resentments. She was sixteen, just returned from a visit to her father and his newest bride. So, how *is* your father? Lois asked, by that unwarranted emphasis accusing Jane of having brought the subject up. Even at sixteen Jane knew what her mother didn't want to hear.

"All right, I guess." Picking her way through an old battlefield still pocked with land mines. Venturing cautiously. "He keeps in pretty good shape."

"What's she like, this latest?"

Jane blinked, seeing a seriation of brides descending Duchamp=s staircase. "All right, I guess. I mean, for Chrissake, I was just down there for a week. She was nice enough. For someone with all that money, I mean. I don't care much for their friends."

"I hear your father's having a transplant."

"My God! Oh no! We played tennis—" Vision of those brown golden-haired thighs imprinted on hard clay, the soles of white sneakers turned up, the death-dealing racquet in her hand.

Lois snickered. "His hair, silly, his hair." Eyed the melting ice in the drink she held, gave the glass a shake, examined the resulting swoosh as if conducting a chemical experiment. Jane watched it too, afraid of an explosion. "Your father, in case you didn't know, was always very vain."

Your father. Erasing her own relationship, leaving it all to Jane. Good news! God punishes by granting your desire. Oh, mother! was Jane's silent plea, but Lois's distant voice denied that relationship as well. The child had always been part of the package.

"Oh, mother," Jane said aloud, with such disgust Lois took it for an expletive.

"What the hell." Lois was addressing her still full glass. "Better vain than plain. Without love, one grows plain. Plain." She sounded drunk but it could only be despair that had unbuttoned her. "You see, I still believe in love."

And what do I believe in, Jane asked herself under the locust tree. Not in love, evidently, or the question would not have formed. In the rights of man? In Individual Retirement Accounts? In holistic medicine? Free choice? U.F.O.'s? Public schools? Global warming? Vitamins and/or psychotherapy? In the Society of Elath? Good God, not *that*, at least!

It struck her that her yeses had always been small-voiced and tentative, only the no's carried true conviction. Was there not one article of faith she could affirm without those shilly-shallying *it depends, under some circumstances, all other things being equal, relatively speaking?*

How funny, she suddenly thought, that in probing for some belief, not one question about religion had occurred to her. *Her* fault, Jane whined (still totting up the score against Lois)—hauling me off to church only in those man-dry depressions between careers, sneaking in on Sundays as surreptitiously as on less holy days she darted into gypsy tearooms, asking much the same advice—Oh, God, *now* what do I do?—and, Jane had noticed in passing the collection plate, crossing the palm with the same silver.

"*You* were lucky." That was Boone, conducting his perennial competition in misery (You think you've got a head cold? I've got atypical pneumonia). "We went every Sunday, and every Sunday all we heard was a critical exercise in deconstruction, with God as the text."

"For all that, you were brought up with a clear sense of right and wrong," she accused him (by which she meant, even then, his yeses were as unequivocal as her no's).

"If you mean ethics—" as if they were table manners, she remembered now his shrug—"who needs the Bible when there's Dr. Seuss?"

So why, Boone, do you return now from that weed-patch as if you had been walking in the vineyards of the Lord? At the feast—that's all they were waiting for, she was sure—she and Boone would be asked to take the Vow. And if things went on the way they were, Boone would say yes and she would say no. Always no. She felt cheated—everyone believes in something. Did she believe even that or was she just repeating one of those old adages like blood is thicker than water, beauty is as beauty does, marry in haste and repent in leisure? She fixed her eyes on the unremitting orderly procession of ants, as if therein lay the answer. As a dam, the twig had proved only temporarily disconcerting. She picked it up again, swept it across the ground, up and down and back again, the kind of mad housekeeping that gods went in for. In a flash came the longed-for revelation. The one thing she believed in. Original sin. Now *there* was a rock on which to build a faith! Jane leaned back against the tree with considerable satisfaction. It certainly explained everything on the eleven o'clock news: Star Wars, toxic dumps, child-abusers, bombs bursting in air, crack on the streets, AIDS in the schools, those poor animals found tortured in a zoo. What I have here, she thought, with an exhilaration that ignored all footnote credits, is a unified field theory of the moral universe.

So why was she laughing? (Oh, God, she groaned, those ants are back again.) No doubt a belief so poisonous carried its own antidote or it would kill. Seeing where that led her, Jane laughed all the harder. There was Boone, on his way back to the barn—he would appreciate the joke. She waved energetically, inviting him to join her. I have made a great discovery, Boone, she would greet him—I am one of the Elect! The biggest gamble of them all—salvation unearned, in no way deserved— Jesus's as well as Fortune's child! But before he reached her, she had changed her mind. She was no longer sure what would make him laugh.

"I'm beat," Boone said and plopped down beside her.

"You're sitting on the ants," Jane said. Poor ants, another natural disaster. Boone jumped up, beating his legs, arms, batting his ears. "So. What did you learn about farming today?"

He looked down at her. "The eye of the Master fattens the corn."

She couldn't tell if he was joking or serious. "It's a good thing it's fattened already, you can hardly keep your eye on it if they won't let you out the gate."

"I was talking about the seed plot—the experimental stuff."

"Oh, the weed-patch," she sneered.

"I spent most of the day with guys in the garage. All they talk about is this Feast—but when I ask what it represents, what it's *for*, they shut up. Funny, usually these sects that have the Truth are only too anxious to ram it down your throat."

He was asking questions? Then there was still hope. She held out her arm and he pulled her up. Impulsively she kissed him.

"Thank you," she said bitterly. "You took that like a man."

"I don't know if I want to participate if I don't know what it's all about," he said. It took her a moment to realize he was still talking about the feast. If Boone did not perceive her, did she exist? He was still thinking, so obviously *he* did. "It's like signing a petition without reading it, just because you pass the corner where they're handing it out," he continued as they walked back to the barn.

"Oh, I do that all the time," Jane said. "I remember once there were pickets outside the supermarket, asking us not to buy grapes. Naturally I figured the petition on the corner was something to do with the UFW. Found out later it was for capital punishment." Looking at his back as he walked ahead of her, she was glad she had signed.

"Or like filling out a pledge card for some charity you've never heard of," Boone said, still conversing with himself.

Filling out a pledge card never worried Jane. She never intended to pay anyway. She only did it in a fit of enthusiasm or to spare herself embarrassment. Rather, she thought , the way she had married Boone.

Chapter X

Boone in his eagerness to see the inside of the Dome had set off alone for the party. Jane still could not decide what to wear. No problem for Boone—white t-shirt under high-bibbed overalls, dress version of the Society's uniform—but in spite of his impatient urging, she refused to put on the long calico gown. She remembered, if he did not, that his response the evening she had modeled it was to dump her from his lap.

They had traveled light, shipping most of their clothes along with a few valued possessions, everything else disposed of in a joint apartment sale. (How silly to feel a lump in the throat at the thought of the unwanted Monster once again abandoned on the street.) Nothing she had brought with her seemed appropriately festive or even sufficiently becoming. Searching for the third time through the one little closet, she noticed that the dress left behind by some previous occupant had a proclivity for nesting on the floor. Too slippery to stay on its hanger and, with its bias cut, too susceptible to stretching, it should be laid flat in a drawer. She shook it out, brushed off the dust, and midway in the folding asked herself why not? Such clothes belong to no one here, Melissa had said, disowning it. To Jane the analogy was clear: so had Boone disowned her. Ergo, the dress was bound to fit.

The small mirror over the basin, blotched as with a skin disease, was no help, but she knew from the feel—pure silk, she was sure, although there was no label—that she looked terrific. The color—a rich plum— made her face look less sallow, her eyes almost tawny. It called for high heels, but the gold sandals would do.

She descended rickety stairs, toeing out like a ballerina, thinking: I'll knock them dead. But when she emerged from the old barn and saw the Dome lit up, shyness struck her. She would stick out like a sore thumb. Even as she neared the Dome, she was still considering a change of dress— she could go back and put on the calico and no one would look at her twice.

Indecision had brought her to a halt when, directly behind her, came the stern reprimand: "No loitering, please." She was startled into a little "oh." Rafe—a smiling Rafe—came up beside her. Her pulse still raced, but no longer with fright.

"You're loitering too," she said aggressively. She gripped a denim shoulder strap, pulled him within range of her scent, and looked severe. "Why aren't you in there with the others?"

He made no move to back away or break her grip, but his very stillness served the same purpose. "I had to go check on the alarm—something had run into the fence."

She tightened her grip, using the pretense of nervousness to get closer. "I don't know much about electricity—it scares me. I hope the voltage isn't high enough to kill?" From Melissa's warning, she had gathered the charge was no greater than a cattle prod's, unpleasant but not serious, but ignorance always had its appeal.

"We-ell," he said, as if the matter required some thought, "if you're a dog and lift your leg to pee against it—

"Is that what happened? The poor thing!" She gave a sympathetic shiver for the dog. Transferred the sympathy to him. How awful he must be feeling. Using the pelvic tilt taught in all her exercise classes, she pressed against him in just the right places. He gave no sign of feeling anything.

Her shiver now was real, for oh yes this was the real thing. Here was a heart which would not open, batter and pummel as she would with all the primal fury of her emotions. Much as, when a child, she had eaten first the bad things on her plate, saving for the last the things she liked, she required a foretaste of disaster and then, only then, how she gorged on passion! Once started up, that dynamo of desire she called love would shake her apart—an engine too powerful for the housing of her body. It always happened that way, so why was it was not happening now? She kissed him full on the mouth—an act of desperation.

All was still, all was quiet. Under the denim not even that little flutter like a fledgling's wings being tested for flight.

"Oh, let's go in," she said petulantly, but her disappointment was with herself, that failure of the motor to kick over. She tasted salty blood where, in clamping down against the intrusion of her tongue, he had bitten her lower lip. He must be gay, she excused herself. "Whatever happened to that wife of yours?" she asked with seeming casualness.

"What you're really asking is am I gay." His smile irked her with its condescension. "For what it's worth, when I came here I was not only married, but happily as they say. Not that I knew what marriage was until I joined the Society. Pardon the expression—" his smile broadened—"but it took The Windigo to straighten me out."

She looked at him curiously. Really married, then. He had chosen to answer only her unspoken question but she knew who was the wife in question. Her first impressions were always right.

"Spare me the details of your conversion," she said. "I'm not interested in taking any more vows." Immediately regretting her snippiness, she took his arm. "But thank you for walking in with me. I hate entering a party alone."

"Oh, sure," he said, "my pleasure," although there was little sign of that in his demeanor. They might be walking arm in arm but he had removed himself beyond her reach. If this were the old Jane, she would have been by now in a full-blown tantrum of love, and life—that old black-and-white film—would have switched into full living color. Sick, sick, sick—so all her friends had scolded her. But this new Jane—a body invaded by an alien?—looked at the distanced man beside her and found him a bore. Strange, after so many years of chronic illness, to be suddenly stricken with health. She took a deep breath, expecting to feel the oxygen-high of an early-morning jogger. The breath was expelled as a jagged sigh. Was this all health amounted to—the dull absence of pain?

Panic seized her. She wanted the old Jane back, who alone (with the early Christians) knew the true meaning of passion: suffering on the cross. She felt as ill at ease with the new Jane as with a stranger whose tastes seemed outlandish and whose habits had already begun to annoy. A dark suspicion surfaced that the change had something to do with being married—that Boone had tricked her into a ceremony that involved more than a convenient way of traveling together. He was sly enough—hadn't he tricked her at the outset by that wedding ring? Not really, she had to confess—it took more than a ring to demark a man as unavailable. He was there for the taking, she had sensed that quickly enough, which was how she could tell he would do only until the real thing came along. Yet what was intended as a brief interlude had dragged on and on. Maybe I do love Boone, she thought despondently—in a healthy sort of way.

Still clutching Rafe's arm, she entered the Dome prepared for invidious glances at her attire, for shocked head-turning at the sudden intrusion of sex into this one big happy family gathering. Not a glance was sent her way; not a head turned. She reached the depressing conclusion that she might as well have worn the calico gown. Then her spirits lifted as she viewed the colored lights, the long trestle table furnished with punch bowl and chunky dark brown cookies, a live band (two guitars and a fiddle) tuning up on a slightly raised podium—all the necessary paraphernalia for gaity. True, the shapeless gowns and stiff overalls were loosely clumped in separate entities but the dancing, about to begin, would mix them.

Another decorative touch added to the party spirit, she now noticed. Colored banners—red, blue, yellow, white—hanging where before the photographs had been displayed. A decided improvement, she judged it. It would be difficult to indulge in any frivolity in the presence of those serious heads.

"I see you've taken down the portraits," she remarked.

"Not taken down," Rafe said. "They're still there. Behind the holy colors. The departed ones are always with us."

"I see. In spirit if not in flesh," Jane quipped. From his sharp look, she realized that levity was a mistake. "Departed *who?*" she asked more respectfully.

"Departed spouses," he said, glancing up at the banners with what she took for a soulful look. Her own glance was in the direction of Melissa. *His* spouse, she almost said, had not departed very far.

As if responding to Jane's attention, Melissa emerged from the female huddle to pounce on Rafe. "I see what took you so long." She was shaking a finger—playfully, Jane assumed but still removed her hand from Rafe's arm with the alarmed jerk of one touching a hotplate.

Everyone smiled here, but no one laughed. Jane had not realized this until now, when for the first time the rule was broken by an explosion from Melissa, who quickly covered her mouth, applying manual control where the automatic had failed. "You really think I am jealous!" she spluttered. "If you only knew how ridiculous that is."

"You see," a more sober Rafe explained, "we have taken the Holy Vow."

Jane looked from one to the other. That, she was forced to conclude, was the full explanation. Melissa, mirth again reduced to a smile, nodded in confirmation. "Oh my dear, if you too were to take it—"

In self-defense Jane scowled. "We really aren't interested—" she began but was brought up short by a sudden doubt if she could speak for Boone.

"Oh, not you two. You too. T-o-o. You mustn't misunderstand."

"Only one of you," Rafe said, again putting a gloss on Melissa's blunt statement. "That's the way it works with couples."

His hermeneutics left much to be desired, Jane was about to retort when something more important occurred to her.

"But you and Melissa—you came here as a couple, didn't you? I certainly had the impression that you two were married."

That broke them up. They hung on each other like two drunks providing mutual support.

"But we all look that way," Melissa was finally able to say. "That's the proof of it, that the Vow really works." Further proof, if needed, was provided by the way they looked at each other—with an ardor that seemed to make shimmering heat waves in the air yet left Jane out in the cold. Whatever vows these two had taken, Jane could see it worked in a way the marriage vows she and Boone had exchanged never would. Jealousy might be forbidden them, but Jane could feel it roiling her insides. Or something was. Could she be coming down with a bug? The flu would be nice, she thought, eager to attribute her malaise to something comfy like a virus.

The guitars had strummed their readiness for the dancing to start. The clumps were breaking up, reforming into another configuration. Jane looked around for Boone. She was willing to stomp and bow, sashay and turn, so long as she could do it one-on-one.

"Oh Boone!" she called, seeing another of those disconcerting flashbacks to a Boone just met—a medium kind of man, of medium height and medium features, who neither promised great possibilities nor foreclosed them. And who wore now a real wedding ring, a tighter fit, with no less an air of disengagement. She closed in on him and demanded, "Dance with me."

Boone dislodged her hand from his sleeve as if plucking off a burr. She covered her embarrassment with a derisive smile as he aligned himself with the men linked at the waist—not for the square dance she had expected but for another folk dance of some sort. On the other side of the room, Melissa held out a hand to her, an invitation to join the women's line. She ignored it and headed straight for the punch bowl. Irene would like it here, Boone had said contemptuously in those early days (it seemed a lifetime they had been here) when he still had sense enough to be contemptuous. But, tasting the innocuous mix of juices, Jane thought not.

Dance with me. Hand clawing on his sleeve. His flesh had shrunk from her touch, remembering what the mind did not. But then the mind caught up: it was the same public gesture of intimacy she had used to present him to her mother. Abused, misused—now as then. The "I love you, Boone," with which she had sought to repair the damage of that weekend had even then been suspect. Then as now.

The long drive upstate, the swooshing along country roads in the throes of a spring thaw, the intimidating prospect of two days in the company of a trio of women—all that he had steeled himself to endure under the delusion it was to be their sole obeisance to convention. I do think you ought to meet my mother, was all Jane had said. Not a word as yet about a church wedding.

This is Boone. She had pulled him toward the taller of the two women with all the ingratiating subtlety of Irene's cat depositing a dead mole at the feet of her beloved. (I'm the one who feeds her, Irene complained, you don't even like cats, but she brings them to you.) And this is Little Missy, he told himself, but did not believe it. Emerging from her embrace, he had sought in that ungainly splay-footed woman, thin and shoulder-hunched, some vestige of the child star. The once dark hair was of a lighter, almost metallic hue, as if immortalized in bronze like a pair of baby shoes. No more Dutch-boy bob, of course; instead a stiff upward brush, short straight hair standing on end all around her head—a style Boone had always thought a cartoonist's convention signifying a state of extreme horror or fear. The unformed putty of the child's face had lengthened, developed bone, and whatever handsomeness it may have had in young womanhood had settled now into horsy plainness. But the eyes were still there, those super-nova eyes that had glowed on the screen, not quite so out-sized in the grosser setting of maturity but still fixing the viewer with the intensity of their gaze. A slight nystagmus, shunting the irises from side to side, had her reading his face as if it were a written text. Just so had Little Missy looked up at Billy Drood, searching for some clue to grown-up thought, some explication of grown-up emotion. One difference: this six-footer was looking down, not up.

But what was Little Missy without Billy Drood? "Adele," the much shorter woman said, thrust out a hand, shook his briskly. He was left with the impression they had concluded a business deal. Broad heavy face, broad heavy body. Boone had thought of Amy Lowell, without the cigar.

"Darling," Lois said, kissing her daughter antiseptically on the forehead, and even to Boone the endearment was unconvincing, more like the evasive tactic for a name unrecalled. "You never mentioned he was actually good-looking. And so—so presentable, compared to your usual—" Over the hand stopping her mouth, Little Missy's eyes search their faces for some sign of devastation. In her films, at least, that was the inevitable result of the child speaking truth. Her acting, Boone took note, had not improved.

As for Adele, no acting there. If her handshake was a business deal, he had the worst of it, she made clear. In his discomfort he focused on the roll of posters clutched under her arm. Black letters on orange. No Hunting, he decoded and ventured a sociable remark.

"I suppose there're a lot of deer up here."

He discovered that light grey eyes could have the property of dry ice, smoking and freezing at the same time. "In case you're thinking of coming up here for the season, you should know I intend to back these up with a shotgun."

"She's a crack shot too," Lois said proudly.

Quickly he disavowed any interest in hunting, which put an end to her interest in him. Jane and only Jane stood before her, to be welcomed with those warm maternal recriminations ("We never see you, why can't you stay longer? You're looking peaked, isn't that a cold sore on your mouth?") that Jane's own mother seemed incapable of. Jane squirmed like a kitten petted against its will, not yet inured to the constraints of human affection.

"Sorry, must go," Adele said, slapping the roll of posters into her open palm. To Jane went the apology, the slap to him. "Want to get these up before dark."

Determined to do right by his Jane, he offered to help nail them up. Which merited him another icy look. Trees were living sentient beings (unlike hunters, he made note). How would he like nails hammered into him?

Jesus Christ, he muttered, and Jane gave him a warning kick and Adele strode off.

"Why do you think she had a coil of wire on her shoulder?" Jane asked, dissociating herself from him with a superior smile. She was letting him know again that she was more sensitive than he to the needs of others. Including trees.

"I saw the wire," he countered. "I was using 'nail' figuratively, meaning 'to affix.' As in: he nailed her to the wall."

"Hah," Jane said. A morose threesome now, they sloshed through the sodden mulch of last year's leaves toward the house. Built according to Adele's own plans, Lois said, perking up a bit; all post and beam, not a nail in the entire construction.

Something caught on his trousers, something pounced on his lifted foot. They were walking through a thicket of cats. Jane had no scruples about kicking them away ("Scat, McKinley! You too, Garfield!), but he doubted he had the same prerogative, not having been formally introduced. Instead he adopted a shambling gait, hoping the thrust of his leg would dislodge the claws caught, fortunately, in corduroy not flesh.

"It's stuck, poor thing," Lois said and kneeled at his feet. "There, they're out. Harrison's always getting stuck like that, there must be something wrong with his nails."

To Boone's ear, 'nail' was beginning to have the nonsense sound of a word too often repeated.

"Oh, no, you don't, Harrison," Lois scolded. "You know perfectly well only Wilkie is allowed inside." She blocked off the mangy-looking grey with her leg, shooed Boone and Jane inside. It was Wilkie, he presumed, who, in the posture of a doorstop, greeted him with unblinking yellow-eyed stare. A coat of many colors, randomly stitched.

"He's a handsome one," Boone said insincerely.

"It's a she," Jane said. "Politics, not gender, is the key. You've yet to meet Coolidge, Taft, Hays, TR—he uses his initials so as not to be confused with you-know-who. How many is that? Whom have I left out, Lois?"

He looked at Wilkie with renewed interest. The only loser. "What about him?"

"Her," Jane corrected impatiently.

"No, him—Wilkie. He doesn't fit in that list."

"Oh, him. That's easy. Once, when Adele was just a little girl, her daddy brought Mr. Wilkie home to dinner, and she fell in love. Permanently, it would seem."

Boone turned to Lois for confirmation. She giggled. "Don't look at me. They're Adele's cats."

"And this," Jane said, sounding as neutered as a tour guide, "is Adele's house. What do you think?"

The question was a nudge to look about him. Admittedly he was not usually attentive to his surroundings. After two years, on and off, sleeping in Jane's apartment, he still could not maneuver in the dark without bumping his shins. And all he was to remember of this post-and-beam structure were the beams—mammoth spans of some giant species of a tree. And Little Missy simpering at him from the walls. Surely these movie stills were a more permanent embarrassment than the films Jane's father had sporadically run, but Lois gave no evidence of seeing them at all. No room divisions on this floor, just a barn-like space, cozied by comfortable furniture and worn orientals underfoot, large ones overlapping, small ones on top of them, as if thrown down by a bazaar merchant to display all his wares. Lois's pride was evidently in the rear, where the kitchen announced itself by a chandelier of copper pots and a black wood-burning stove and—she confessed this was her particular delight—a walk-out greenhouse from which she plucked a sprig of rosemary and placed it in his jacket buttonhole.

Once up the stairs to a corridor of bedroom doors, Jane lost no time in vanishing (last door, he took note) but he was braked by Lois pulling on his arm. Look, she demanded, turning him to face the wall. Early American primitive, he judged the two half-length portraits, painted on wood panels by one of those itinerant artists who would also do the barn. There was a certain charm in the clumsy yet faithful rendering of the faces—the cast in the woman's right eye, the man's knobby chin and sharp Adam's apple—but the heads did not fit the prefab torsos. It made him think of an amusement park photo he and Jane had once taken, his head resting on the cardboard cutout of Superman's body, bulging in all the right places, and Jane's, with lids lowered at half-mast and a pursed-up mouth, rearing above the curves, equally bulging but in different places, of Marilyn Monroe. Remembering that failed attempt at sultriness—it was the look his mother wore when trying to thread a needle without her glasses—he felt an attack of tenderness, unsettling as nausea.

He became aware that he was being introduced. "Adele's great great—" for a moment Lois looked confused and then, like Jane in the kitchen, threw in another "great" for good measure—"great-grandparents. Adele doesn't like me to talk about it, but the Lanyards are a very old family, they go back to the seventeenth century—the American branch, that is."

She was whispering, as if divulging some scandalous secret. He whispered back that he wouldn't mention it to a soul. She looked at him doubtfully—was he laughing at her? He could not bear Little Missy's eyes rebuking him and made amends by expressing more interest than he felt in these forbears of her friend. He was still being filled in on past Lanyard notables—a Supreme Court justice, a governor, a Union general, a bank president, a brace of cabinet members—when she opened his bedroom door. Not the last, the penultimate door.

Impatiently waiting for her to leave while she ran through her role of perfect hostess, he amused himself by providing the bracketed instructions on her script: (Inspects jonquils in blue bowl for signs of wilting) "Jane tells me you smoke—but I hope not in bed?" (Moves ashtray from night table to dresser stage left.) "If you get cold—" (Opens closet to show where extra blankets can be found.) "And this is the bathroom—I'm sure you don't mind sharing it with Jane?"

He nodded no, he didn't mind. He didn't mind if after two years of living in and out of each other's apartment, if after God knew how many of those less presentable lovers, Jane was still to be accommodated as a virgin.

Lois sat on the bed, patted the space beside her. He could tell the script had changed, but what was she playing now? She waited until he had sat where ordered to say, "Jane tells me you're getting married."

He nodded yes, feeling ornery enough not to break the long silence that followed. She was now playing the mother, that was clear, but had forgotten her lines. "I know there're lots of things I should ask you," she finally said, "but there's one thing I really want to know." She took his hand, fixed her eyes on him. "Do you love her?"

The way she said "love"—as if it were a Calvinistic transport by which he would know he had been "saved"—the leech-like suction of her gaze made him squirm. He managed to look away, half expecting to hear a pop as their eyes disengaged, and muttered something. Whatever he had said, the word "love" wasn't in it.

As soon as the door closed behind her, he used the bathroom passage to Jane's room. Sitting on the edge of the bed, shoulders rounded, hands dangling between her knees, she was a subject for a Hopper painting, remote and separate from both her surroundings and any other human in the scene. Namely, him. He had entered expecting the question: so what do you think of my mother? To that he had a diplomatic answer prepared, but she had thrown him off-stride by asking instead: so what do you think of Adele?

He was as shocked as she when that word came out of his mouth. Even so, it didn't excuse such a tantrum, angry accusations hurled like crockery at his head. Unable to defend himself, he had done the next best thing, made a dignified exit. A cigarette smoked in the bathroom—a safe distance from any inflammable substance—calmed him enough to reconsider his position. It was a long weekend that lay ahead. He went back in to apologize.

She too had reconsidered her position. She now lay supine on the bed, arms and legs stretched out like some luckless explorer pegged down by a savage tribe as honeyed offering to army ants. Five minutes with her mother and she was already a basket case. He felt an equal mix of sympathy and annoyance. Why had she insisted on this trip? The kind of City Hall ceremony he had in mind—he pictured an ambience something like that of the Motor Vehicle Bureau—hardly required a mother's blessing. In lieu of the absent wedding ring (oh no you don't, Jane had said when they had ended up again in bed, not until you get rid of that and I mean permanently this time), he rubbed the knuckle of the bare finger. Without the smooth slippage of gold against his skin, there was no pacifying effect, only a dry friction.

"You know what your mother asked me? " he said, hearing himself cajole a sulky child. "Do I love you, she wanted to know. I didn't let on, of course, but I guess I do."

She had said nothing then, merely looked up at him askance. Yet on the drive back to the city, she had broken a long silence with that astonishing announcement: "I want a real wedding, in a real church, with a real minister and a real service."

She's crazy, he thought, but "okay" was all he said. Still she must have felt a need to explain this sudden change in plans. "I love you, Boone," she said with a vehemence that implied someone had denied it, so startling him that he veered onto the shoulder of the road. At times he thought she did, but that was not one of them.

Nor was this, he thought, abandoning himself to the male-bonding of those arms around his waist.

Boone, who had always felt a fool when required to move his body rhythmically, was discovering he could dance. This kind of dance, he qualified—in a line never broken, now side by side, now front to rear, now stomping forward, now sliding backward, now a sidewinder's slithering along a diagonal. Yet, however varied the movement, always as a single organism. Across the room, the women's line mirrored their every step, adding the extra fillip of flouncing skirts.

At a table pushed back against the wall, The Windigo sat alone, stocky thighs spread wide, surveying the two lines of dancers with the same complacent smile he had addressed to his plot of seed corn. He looks upon his work and finds it good—a thought sufficiently satirical to wrench Boone out of synch with his fellows. Returned to awkwardness, he grew more critical. A mindless ability, moving as one. Nature had engineered this kind of thing before—a creature of many fused segments, each bearing two legs, living primarily on vegetable—rarely animal—matter, whose only defense was an unpleasant body odor. Class: Diplopoda. Amusement at the thought of a dancing millipede gave way to a more conscious awareness of the acrid stink exuded by his neighbors. Sweat was to be expected with all this exertion, but these were the same men who in digging a barbecue pit in the midday sun had jokingly held their noses in his proximity, who had asserted—still joking, of course—that their own lack of odor, without benefit of deodorants, proved them a superior kind of being, pure and incontaminate. Cautiously he sniffed his own armpit, was relieved that now their odor outranked his. Revulsion gave him the impetus to break free of the line. The millipede, cut in two, immediately fused its broken ends, healing itself in the way of such primitive life forms.

"It's the meat."

Boone gaped, startled by The Windigo's undetected approach. The Windigo raised his arm—dance with me? was Boone's first appalled reading of the gesture—then sniffed, a Rabelaisian sniff that made a vacuum-cleaning noise. Boone relieved himself with a manic burst of laughter.

The Windigo seemed pleased at the effectiveness of his performance. "You find the odor unpleasant? When we return to our normal diet, it will disappear."

Boone said skeptically, "I see." He had eaten meat all his life without emitting such a stench.

"What is it you do not see?" The Windigo probed gently.

"Well, that doesn't seem to apply to me," Boone said, with the arrogance of the non-odorous.

"Ah, but you have been with us for so short a time, your body has not yet adjusted to our regime."

"I see," Boone said, making the preparatory movement of one about to leave.

"Nor have you taken the Vow," The Windigo said, holding him by the overall strap. "To those who have, that smell—to you a stink—is the sweetest smell of all, the very immanence of Elath, proof that his spirit is within us on these Feast days."

Turning skittish, like an animal flaring its nostrils, pricking its ears in instinctive alarm, Boone pulled free, muttered something about finding Jane. He liked this ordered life, yet at the first pressure on him to join, he felt like yelling no! I won't! I won't!

The boy's just plain contrary. His mother speaking, and from somewhere outside his head. It was not the first time he had heard that disembodied voice. Like a radio signal from a far-distant station that because of some atmospheric disturbance suddenly comes in clear and strong, her voice would cut through the static of the moment, ring out his name. *Boone!* he had first heard her call on a sweltering summer afternoon just outside Nimes. (That had been his high-school graduation present—a biking trip through France. On a postcard he had asked: Were you thinking of me at 2:00 p.m. (9:00 a.m. your time) last Sunday afternoon? I'm always thinking of you, dear, was the reply awaiting him in Paris at American

Express.) Another *Boone!* had given him a guilty start on his first camping trip with Jane. A *Boone!* had even reached him 20,000 feet above the earth. Boone!—just his name. But now that she was dead, she had grown loquacious, he was hearing whole sentences. *The boy's just plain contrary, he said he had a good time at the farm and now his Uncle Eban wants him back, he's screaming he won't go.*

Looking up at the string of colored lights, Boone felt a desperate need for fresh air. The guitars still strummed, the fiddle scraped, the dancers stomped but all at a distant remove. He looked around for Jane. She was nowhere to be seen. Was there something in the spirit of this place or in the state of matrimony itself that had the one reaching out, the other falling back in a repetitive movement as formalized as any folk dance?

Skirting the dancers, he made his way to the door and once outside drank in the warm night air in quick shallow gasps. As if he had been running down three flights of stairs. As if he had seen a ghost—not of a person but of a house. The house which once had stood on this spot— built of wood and nails (not post and beam), careless of design, subject to rot and decay, finally destroyed by fire—yet with an afterlife fated to outlast the tetrahedral strength of this new structure. It too had had its colored lights—the little round window in the crow's nest, paned in yellow and purple glass.

Yellow and purple. It was midday but through that window the light was forever a dying afternoon's. From his aerie, he was looking down on the squashed porkpie hat, never doffed indoors or out. Uncle Eban, cleaning out the cowshed by himself. The usual overalls, flailed into pale blue lifelessness by Aunt Flo's laundering, had been replaced by the old denim shirt and trousers kept hanging in the barn for just such jobs. The first time he went inside, Boone had brushed against them, jumped back in alarm, not recognizing them as clothes to be worn. On his uncle, mounding the manure into a dark volcanic cone, they seemed made not of cloth but of some old dark metal, heavy and durable as iron, as seasoned in their way as the skillet on Aunt Flo's stove.

It was Aunt Flo's entrance that gave the scene a disconcerting turn. She was wearing a too-large raincoat of smoky transparency, strange stuff that reminded Boone of the isinglass windows on the ancient car rusting in the barn. Why a raincoat? was the puzzle. Boone peered up. Not a cloud in the yellow sky. Not a shadow of a cloud near the purple sun. Squeezed tightly under her arm, a plump chicken squirmed. Its beak took chopstick bites out of empty air. A frisson of terror—or was it delight?—rippled over

Boone's skin. He knew, even as the chicken seemed to know, what came next.

I'll wring your neck. Her customary expression of mild annoyance. *You track mud over this floor just one more time, boy, I'll wring your neck.*

The boy remembered back to breakfast, what she had said. Not for you to watch, don't even let the other chickens watch, she had said. All he heard from Uncle Eban was a contemptuous expulsion of air through the hairy marshland in his nose, but shut up, Aunt Flo commanded, taking a steel hairpin out of her hair and glaring across the table as if she meant to plunge it into Uncle Eban's heart, stuck it instead into another part of her scalp. It's not like the boy's brought up to it, she said. Take me, it's been my chore since I was eight years old, when Ma got her bursitis. My sister Edna now, she never done it till she was married. You should have seen her, boy, that first time. She left her new husband high and dry, with no supper on the stove, come crying home to Ma and me, all covered with the blood.

Uncle Eban addressed a snort to "your sister Edna," but Aunt Flo's patting of her thick grey hair, her groping for the lethal hairpin was purely automatic. Hers was the foolish out-of-focus smile that grownups wore when remembering good times past. Poor Edna, she had laughed.

Poor chicken. Boone heard the furious pounding of the tiny heart under the feathered breast. It took the silent mouthing of the figures far below to make him realize the heartbeat was his own. They were yelling. The mouths spat and twisted and opened wide in silent roars. He could hear nothing. He was missing all the fight. He wiped the stained glass porthole with his shirttail as if cleaning wax out of his ears. Uncle Eban flung his shovel to the ground and yelled again. One hand still binding tight the chicken's legs, Aunt Flo used her other to tear into her hair, jerking out, jabbing in the pins, her mouth working away. When it happened it took him completely by surprise. Reversing her hold, its head now in her hand, she began to whirl the chicken around and around, the way he whirled his model planes into flight. Oh ho, he's going to get it now, Boone laughed to himself, as silently as those titans cursing each other below—she's going to throw it at him. And so she did.

The chicken took off straight for Uncle Eban, but its head stayed in her hand. Boone saw the reason for the raincoat then. Uncle Eban was soaked with blood, stunned with blood. Aunt Flo's head was far back, her mouth open, drowning in laughter. The chicken kept on going, floundering about the bare yard, a geyser of blood spouting from the open neck, its wings flapping vigorously as if still convinced it could escape in flight. He did not see Uncle Eban scoop up a shovelful but he heard Aunt Flo's scream, faint and shrill as a train whistle miles down the track.

Uncle Eban dripping with blood. Aunt Flo covered with that other stuff. In her hair, plastered to her face, oozing from her mouth. And the chicken careening around them both, its blood now jetting in a finer spray, a lawnsprinkler wetting the thirsty earth in a time of drought.

Chapter XI

Jane heard him climbing the stairs, pulled up the sheet she had kicked off and lay in wait. 1) Pretend to be asleep. 2) Allow yourself to be awakened by the noise he makes (refer to lack of consideration). 3) Deliver a few pungent remarks on the party: that cool-aid version of a punch, the inedibly healthful cookies, the hokey music, the no-touch dancing. Which you seemed to enjoy so much, she rehearsed, although it's true you're not much of a dancer.

It was hard lying in wait when he was taking his own sweet time. If this were a horror movie, she thought, she would be petrified by that slow approach. And those pauses. Another few creaks, then another pause, surely near the top now? Eyes closed, she tried to visualize where he was standing. What she saw was Uncle Eban swinging from the rafter.

"What took you so long?" she cried with relief as soon as he turned on the light. "I've been waiting up for you." So much for rehearsals.

An indecipherable grunt. He collapsed on the bed and relief gave way to concern. Jane moved over to perch on the metal rim, careful not to encroach on the mattress— an automatic, though still measured, response to his evident need for comforting, putting on hold (but by no means disconnecting) her own neediness, not forgetting, even as she patted his head (impossible to stroke a rough bristle), to resent the fact that he was always outdoing her: her bad colds, his pneumonias; her sulking discontent, his soul-searing crisis.

"What's the matter, hon? You can't be drunk—not on that punch." She wished he were drunk, she could stand a little affectionate nuzzling. "Whatever it is, you look awful—like you've seen a ghost."

"I have," he said and flung his arm across his face.

Then he had visualized it too—Uncle Eban, swinging from the rafter? She felt a premonitory thrill at the thought of the same image occurring to them at the same time—that's what happened when you were really married. Just to make sure they were on the same wave length, she said, all but chirping with cheerfulness, "Funny, a few minutes ago, before you came in, I had this mental image of your Uncle Eban?" The question mark quivered in the air while she waited for the answer that would determine their future happiness.

"So did I," he said.

"Oh, Boone," she sighed, feeling as if she had had her fortune told by a favorably disposed gypsy. She pulled his arm away to pepper him with kisses, fierce little smacks wherever flesh was exposed—brow and nose, cheek and chin, collarbone. Marking my territory, she thought, as she surveyed the passive terrain stretched beneath her. His eyes were closed— was it to concentrate the pleasure? An exploratory touch destroyed that illusion. All calm, all quiet. She had moved out of the house of her past, ready to move in with him, only to find another shut door. Translating ungovernable rage into unassuageable desire, she tore open his fly, rubbed his limp cock between her palms. A ludicrous image leaped to mind: herself as Girl Scout, twirling a dry stick, trying to ignite a fire. If she remembered rightly, she had failed at that, too.

A shudder spread through the body she was woman-handling. "What the hell are you doing?" Boone cried out. Flinging her aside, he got groggily to his feet, staggered as he zipped himself up, knocked over a nearby chair. He righted the chair but she noticed that her jeans and shirt, tossed on the seat when she was dressing for the party, were left on the floor.

"Pick them up! You're not to leave my things on the floor."

He obeyed her, an automaton responding to remote control. From the pocket of her shirt, picked up by the tail, fell a cache of corn kernels, scattering like buckshot across the bare floor. He stared at them in confusion, then recognized their provenance.

"You're not supposed to take extras," he said dully, "they're part of the ritual, not something to snack on."

Even his disapproval sounded programmed. She gave a bark of contemptuous laughter. "Those aren't extras, they're my daily allotment. Personally, I can't stand that stuff." And because he seemed genuinely shocked, she condescended to add, "Don't worry, I'm very careful not to offend. I spit them out into my napkin, so no one knows."

Confronted with his troubled wide-eyed look, she could not hold on to her anger. An awkwardness took its place—that of two strangers caught eyeing each other, both quickly looking away. She noticed with what exquisite care he was obeying her instructions—folding her jeans, then her shirt, using the edge of his palm to make sharp creases, as if packing for a trip. Although to judge by his abstracted look, he had already left on one.

"Damn your Uncle Eban!" she exploded. "I wish we had never come here. I wish he had never left this place to you. He should have left it to Irene—we'd all be better off."

"Don't." The cry was no more than a soft whisper, but it stopped her cold. Shoulders hunched, holding his head between his hands, he collapsed into the chair. "A headache," he mumbled; retching with pain, gasped, "Like someone doing laser surgery on my brain." It sounded like a migraine, she reassured them both, and rushed into the bathroom for some aspirin, returned to find him on the bed, sheet pulled over his head. To her urging to lift himself so he could swallow, no response. Her own heart seemed to stop as she uncovered him. His pulse was steady, his color good, his breathing regular. "Are you asleep, Boone?" she prodded. There he lay, comfortably passed out, and she almost dead from fright. "I could kill you," she muttered, and turned out the light.

He awoke into a blackness both of space and time. Irene. A five-letter word, not yet a name. His throat felt dry. The middle of the night? No, later. He could distinguish the sky framed by the window—its blackness fainting away.

A body in the other bed. Irene. No, Jane. Wife. Farm. Uncle Eban dead. Irene.

He was in the crow's nest, Irene beside him. And below, Uncle Eban dripping blood, Aunt Flo coated in manure. Their furious mouthing. He knew what was being said. Because he could read their lips? Because of what Irene was whispering in his ear?

Are you asleep, Boone? Of course he was asleep, he knew what was up. Uncle Eban wanted him in that stinking barn. Trust Irene to find him, when they had given up. Let her slap him, yell his name, shake him until his teeth rattled—so long as he kept sleeping, she couldn't pass the message on. But she didn't yell or slap, she didn't even shake him. It occurred to him she wasn't trying very hard to wake him. He began to listen to the whispering in his ear. She knew something he didn't know, she would show him. Uncle Eban's—yuk! But a little one would fit just right. Then his shorts were open, she was rubbing his peter, still whispering but getting madder by the minute. Come on, stupid, come on, stupid! He decided he'd rather clean the barn. Mumbling, yawning, stretching, he gave her plenty of warning that he was waking up. In a flash, she was gone. I've got to pee, he thought, but couldn't bring himself to move.

Aunt Flo, still wet from her shower, at the bottom of the stairs. "Where's that girl gone? I want her to shell them peas." Trying to sidle past, he mumbles, "I dunno." She stares hard. "You've wet your pants, a big boy like you," she sneers. "Shame, shame, shame!"

The blinding pain. Sleep falling like a blow on the head. He was awake now, memory intact. And the shame. A tidal wave of shame sucking him under—a fever of shame burning him up. The waves receded, the fever abated, as the twenty years were allowed to pass. And there was Irene, on the doorstep of their father's house, hugging herself for warmth, while he moved her in. The abandoned child. Her eyes accused him: the one who remembers is always abandoned by the one who forgets.

To survive, you *have* to forget, he told himself fiercely and turned toward Jane. He could see her more distinctly now, curled up in sleep. She wished they had never come here, but she was wrong. Still it was not a place he wanted to stay. The Society had given up on Jane, he sensed; he was the one counted on to take the Vow and remain. But things didn't always work according to plan. Not even the seed corn, so strictly manipulated. Hadn't The Windigo remarked that sometimes the results were not as predicted, the plant that grew seemed unrelated to both corn as it is and corn as it was?

He wondered if it were he or Jane who had pulled the beds apart. A pity, he wanted to hold her. The faint prickle of desire vanished as soon as he focused on it. The alarm began to ring.

The clay bowls were passed down the table in habit-smooth ritual, signifying the end of breakfast. When his turn came, Boone reached for the dried kernels with his usual alacrity, a movement that froze in mid-air, to be resumed with an embarrassing clumsiness. He had trouble picking out the four colors, his fingers too thick, too grossly coordinated for such a micromanipulator's job. He caught Jane dabbing mouth with napkin, was annoyed no less now that he knew it was an act. Why so sneaky? Why not come right out and say no, thank you, I'll pass.

The fumbling stopped. He withdrew his hand empty, fingers restored to normal size. "No, thank you," he said to Rafe, "I'll pass."

Surprise traveled like a shock wave up the table to be absorbed in the placid bulk of The Windigo, who merely nodded. "May I ask why?" he called down. "It seemed that you had a particular fondness for them until now."

"They don't agree with me," Boone said and looked so pugnacious that Jane murmured "Boone!" in the tone that meant down, Rover, down.

The Windigo smiled. The smile moved down the table. Jane smiled too—a dab of a smile as deceitful as that dab with the napkin. Boone felt heroic, the only one brandishing a barbative scowl.

When the men emerged from the dining hut, the women were still milling about, a tremor of indecision moving through them. Like a herd on jittery edge, Boone thought, and wondered if a loud handclap would make them stampede. Nor did the men stride off with their usual purposefulness, with Boone wordlessly assigned to one contingent or another. Instead they were hanging about like a platoon waiting to be mustered.

Jane caught his eye and mouthed something. His vision was suddenly blurred by the overlay of Aunt Flo's contorted lips: *You touch that girl again . . . wring your neck . . .* Jane mouthed something again. At that moment The Windigo came out, Rafe at his side. Nodded to his left, nodded to his right. To his disciples all was clear. Coagulating into small clumps, they began to move away, Jane pulled along by Carla and Melissa. On his shoulders, Boone felt the heavy weight of Rafe's friendly arm. Jane's last effort was a pleading look over her shoulder, a directional nod toward the barn. He nodded: gotcha. She wanted to see him, alone, in their quarters.

How can a man be so stupid? Since Boone was already on his way to the machine shop, Jane addressed the purely rhetorical question to herself. He seemed perfectly oblivious to the danger signals she was picking up since his provocative refusal to eat the corn. Not that he should have eaten it—enlightenment had struck them both at the same moment last night: something in those kernels had a mind-altering effect —but why couldn't he follow her lead and simply pretend to? Suffering Carla's friendly squeeze, even manufacturing an appreciative smile, she granted that as a woman, for whom pretense was a survival tactic, she had the advantage there.

She entered the kitchen seemingly eager to be put to work but already plotting how to get away without setting off another alarm. The tasks Carla gave her were boringly routine—the washing up, the scrubbing down—while the others were making constant trips to the Dome, returning with a salacious glow. Melissa, having carried over an armful of freshly ironed table linen, was now awaiting with impatience the dinnerware Jane was washing. No soap, Jane had been instructed, just clear water. Terra-cotta plates, or were they bowls? The rims were high enough. Made of the same stuff as the little bowls in which the corn kernels were served, but glazed inside.

"I haven't seen these before," Jane remarked to Melissa, who was snatching each washed one to dry and stack. "Are they for soup?"

"No," Melissa said, her breath against Jane's neck warm and sweet-smelling. "At the final Feast, we serve Elath his special dish." And because Jane held fast to the last of the set, pressing her with a still-questioning look, she added impatiently, "A kind of stew," at which Jane made a face. She didn't like stew.

"You can't carry all of these," Jane said, handing over the last one. "They're too heavy for one trip, let me help you." All these bustling preparations, the excitement like an electric charge in the air, had made her eager to see the festive arrangements inside the Dome.

The plates were indeed heavy, no wonder Melissa had so quickly agreed to her offer. Melissa set her usual brisk pace and, as usual, Jane struggled to keep up. Not quite successfully. At the entrance to the Dome, Melissa patiently awaited her.

"Thank you, Jane, just put those down and open the door, won't you?"

Obediently Jane freed her arms and turned the knob, only to be issued a contrary command. "Stop right there." Into the sliver of an opening, too narrow to afford even a look inside, Melissa had stuck a foot. "No, Jane, just leave those on the ground, I'll come back out and pick them up." And with a dismissive smile, she slipped quickly through, shutting the door behind her.

In my face! Jane raged. A door slammed like that regressed her faster than any hypnotist's finger snap. She had to fight the urge to hammer with her fists, to kick with her feet. *Let me in! Don't shut me out!*—the wail echoed through some dark corridor of her mind. Approaching footsteps inside. Melissa returning for the rest of the plates? Jane quickly walked away, not to be caught like a child in a sulking fit, still hanging about.

She was halfway back to the kitchen before reality drenched her like a cold shower, extinguishing the firestorm of rage. She was remembering to be afraid. Afraid of what, Boone would ask. *I don't know,* she would have to say. It was like being infected with a virus not yet identified. She knew the exact moment it had invaded her system: at breakfast, when The Windigo had smiled. A smile, passed down from face to face, like another ritual in which she had to pretend to partake.

We've got to get out of here! A silent cry of panic directed across the empty field at Boone. Telepathy was not his strong suit, she thought wryly, remembering how obtusely he had ignored her danger signals . Which was why she had to talk to him. A god-sent opportunity, her exclusion from the Dome. Now was the time to slip off unnoticed to the barn.

Giving the kitchen a wide berth, she hurried to her rendezvous with a faster heart rate than could be explained by her brisk pace. Something had changed since this morning to invalidate their privileged status as guests—a watchfulness turned oppressive, leading in turn to this sneakiness in her own behavior.

Boone was not upstairs in their quarters. Nor, from the limited view afforded by the window, was he in sight. Unable to sit still, she moved from chair to bed to window—still no Boone—back to chair, then on her feet again, itchy with the need for some definitive action. Bags packed and ready to go—that would drive her point home. Empty luggage spread open on the bed, she tore through the room, emptying drawers, denuding the closet, cramming everything into the two bags, no discriminating between his and hers.

Still no Boone. Was there a deliberate effort being made to keep them apart? Paranoia, she rebuked herself—the projection of enemies within onto the world without. But in any case, she would no longer sit here waiting for him to show up, she would go out and find him.

Into the back pockets of her jeans she stuffed both their wallets. A quick look around reassured her that everything else was packed. In the drawers, only the silk jersey, neatly folded, provenance still unknown. In the closet, only the calico gown awaiting some other female novitiate. An idea occurred to her—devilishly clever, she thought it. Only one of any couple was the Society's recruiting policy and until this morning that one was evidently Boone. His apostasy had thrown them into utter confusion. If she put on this dress, thereby adopting their uniform, she would confuse them even more. And since for all they knew she had been regularly ingesting the ritual kernels, they might even see her as Boone's replacement.

The change was quickly made, the discarded jeans tossed on top of the silk jersey, a lewd entanglement that made her grin as she closed the drawer. Whether it was the camouflage of the calico dress or the reassuring weight of the two wallets now resting in its deep pockets, she felt more confident as she headed toward the stairs. Noises below made her call out hopefully, "Boone?" She rushed down, landing almost in the arms of the man she called "the curly-haired one." From the cavernous rear of the barn emerged "the fat one," whom she had noticed as the only hold-out (The Windigo always excepted) against the slimming effects of a vegetarian diet. Not for the first time, she regretted that the seclusion of the sexes had not allowed for formal introductions.

"Oh, it's you," she said vaguely, "I didn't know anyone was down here."

"We didn't know anyone was up there," said the curly-haired one.

Her dress had not escaped their notice. She was glad to see the looks they exchanged were definitely confused ones. But it was disconcerting, the uneasy way they backed away from her, until she remembered that during these feast days they were forbidden to be alone with a female. "What are you doing here?" she asked to prolong the encounter, finding a malicious enjoyment in their discomfort.

It took them a moment of fidgeting, another exchange of looks, to settle on a spokesman. "Wasps," the fat one said, "their nests are all over the rafters."

Jane looked up nervously, crossing her arms and shrinking into a self-hug, as if to offer a smaller target. "I . . . I never noticed them."

It would be dusk before they returned to their nests, she was assured. After which, the barn would be sealed shut and the insecticide bombs, which they were positioning now, set off by remote control.

"Hey, what about us?" Jane protested.

"You'll be inconvenienced, I'm afraid," the curly-haired one said agreeably. "The Windigo suggests you spend the night in the dormitory— just the one night, you understand."

Jane longed to tell them she had no intention of spending the night there, or here, or anywhere on this farm. Instead she smiled just as agreeably and went in search of Boone.

As she approached the machine shop, her determination wavered. March right in and pull him out?—in front of the other men?—a more open flouting of their rules than even Boone had been guilty of? That was hardly in accordance with her plan, of which, she was in danger of forgetting, Boone knew nothing. Nor she much more, other than the need for a precipitate departure (as she saw it, she would present the why, Boone the how). She swerved around the machine shop, deciding the wiser course was to wait for the lunch break. Which must be what Boone was waiting for as well.

Heading for the kitchen, she found herself questioning the presence of the two men in the barn. Were there really wasps? And did one set off bombs like that by remote control? More paranoia perhaps, but the fact remained that some other place must be found to talk with Boone unobserved. Deep in thought, abstracted gaze fixed on the distance, she was only subliminally aware of movement by the Dome. A woman exited, advanced in her direction. "Jane!" Carla called out. Jane gave a guilty start, remembering she had not finished her pot-washing duties. "I didn't recognize you at first," Carla said, now abreast of her.

It took the questioning look, the sharp chin pointed at her dress to bring Jane fully to herself. "Oh, this," she said, smoothing the gathered folds, "Melissa wouldn't let me help her in the Dome, so I took the chance to slip into something more comfortable." She looked in the direction from which Carla had come and adopted a wheedling tone. "I don't suppose I could have just a peek in there?"

Carla smiled a no. "I've just had a final look around to make sure all is in order. Once I lock up—" she playfully waved the key under Jane's nose—"no one enters again until the Feast begins tomorrow."

Still, the dress had some effect, Jane thought, as they walked together to the kitchen. Those sideways glances. And twice Carla opened her thin lips to speak, thought better of it. She doesn't know what to think, Jane decided gleefully, so I must prompt her.

"I don't know what got into Boone this morning. I hope The Windigo wasn't offended."

Carla shrugged. "Some feel the inner necessity to follow Elath's commands, some do not."

"I think I'm beginning to," Jane said hesitantly. "A pity that Boone and I are so out of sync—at first he was very drawn to your way of life here, but I was not. Now that I am too, he seems to be drawing back. I have to admit there's something very attractive about the wholeness I sense in you . . . the . . . the . . ."

"The oneness?"

Ah yes, Jane sighed. Oneness. What she had hoped to find in marriage, but realized more and more each day that she and Boone would always be . . . be . . .

"Two?"

Jane was finding it easier than she had expected. Seek and ye shall find the words given you. "Exactly. I know sex requires two, but I am finding I don't require sex. In fact—" she lowered her voice confidentially, allowed a painful pause. To strike the right tone, she imagined herself a Victorian lady, corseted and bustled, suffering exigent demands from her husband. "In fact, when Boone wants to—you know—I find myself thinking of one excuse after another . . ."

She steeled herself to accept Carla's touch, the sympathetic squeeze of her arm. In fact, Carla assured her, she had discovered for herself Elath's teaching—that true union was something deeper than the external rubbing of body on body. Of course, complete acceptance of Elath's truth came only with the taking of the Vow?

Jane took her cue from the rising inflection. "That's what I really want to talk to you about." Carla waited patiently while Jane gave herself a word of caution: don't go overboard, it will be more believable to still have doubts. "I'm not at all sure I want to go that far, but I'm thinking about it, I really am."

"It takes some longer than others to see the truth," Carla said with an encouraging pat.

They entered the kitchen in a silence that Jane hoped could be classified as pregnant. To prove herself no slacker, she went immediately to the sink to finish the large pot abandoned in favor of the plates Melissa had requested her to rinse. Of stainless steel, it hardly required more than a rinse itself and she began to dry it energetically. A beautiful job, if she said so herself, she could see her reflection.

"Where is everybody?" she thought to ask. Usually at lunchtime—a glance at her watch confirmed that it was almost noon—the kitchen was crowded with women but here they were alone. Lifting the pot to polish away some water spots, she could see Carla's distorted image. Standing by the work table, opening a little drawer that flanked a long one. The long one held utensils, Jane knew—ladles and wooden spoons and strainers and such. The little one she had never noticed. Carla's elongated head—a funhouse mirror image—swiveled toward her. Jane polished energetically, while Carla checked that her back was still turned before dropping the key.

"What can I be thinking of?" Carla exclaimed in belated answer to Jane's question. Jane wondered the same. "You will have to take your lunch alone, my dear, The Windigo has called a meeting in the dining hall. Members only, I'm afraid." Promising they would talk more when she returned—Jane would find some sandwiches on the counter—she hurried out.

Jane stowed away the pot, dried her hands, hung the dishtowel on its rack, picked up a sandwich wax-paper wrapped, and from the little drawer removed the key Carla had slipped inside. Light-headed with excitement, she went out to waylay Boone, holding in her hand a stone to kill two birds: the means to satisfy her curiosity and a place to talk undisturbed.

Chapter XII

Boone had not forgotten that Jane wanted to see him, but getting away proved not so easy. The harvester was being readied for operation and Rafe found him indispensable as an extra pair of hands. Why the urgency, Boone could not help but wonder. The corn, he remembered being told, would not be picked for at least a couple of weeks, depending on the weather. Something about the moisture content of the kernels, he recalled vaguely. So why were they working on the machine as if there were no tomorrow?

"I think I'll take a break," Boone announced, having finished with the brake shoes. Sure, Rafe agreed, but would he first just check the gear box oil and top it up. And then it was sure, but first wash those chains in paraffin. And of course replace them. Hey, man, you can't leave them like that, get that SAE 90 and do a good lube job on them. Then it was sure, right after we readjust the slip clutches, they tend to stick after being idle so long. But finally it was sure, if Boone wanted to run over to the barn and pick up some cigarettes (thought you had kicked that habit, Rafe clucked), he was welcome to. It was time for lunch anyway, Rafe added with a grin.

Boone headed briskly for the barn, remarking with some wonder that he had not even noticed he had stopped smoking. A mistake, to use cigarettes as an excuse, for now he felt the deprivation in full force. Maybe it was the ritual corn (take twice a day, with morning and evening meals) that had so painlessly eradicated the need. My God, if you could market it, you'd make a fortune—hadn't he thought something like that before?

"Boone!"

For a moment he did not know where Jane's voice was coming from. Then he saw her, skulking behind the locust tree. She beckoned, he joined her, stumbling over a gnarled extrusion of roots, feeling silly.

"If you think this makes us invisible—" he began in exasperation. This was no time for childish games. "Why didn't you just wait for me in the barn?"

"Unfortunately, it is otherwise occupied. By wasps—or so they say. Two of the guys are in there, setting up bombs. Or so they say."

Boone was hardly listening, he was scowling at her dress. He hated her in it, he suddenly decided, and said as much. It made her look like . . . like . . .

"Like one of them?" Jane looked down at herself with smug satisfaction. That was the idea, she said, to smooth their ruffled feathers after the shock he had given them at breakfast. "Anyway, I know a much better place where we can go and not be disturbed. Just follow me."

It struck Boone that Jane enjoyed being devious. In crossing the field, she kept within its slight hollow, even adopted a Groucho Marx crouch as they came abreast of the dining hall. It suddenly became a familiar game—hadn't he and Irene played cowboys and Indians in this very field although they had gone Jane one better, crawling on their bellies to avoid being seen by Aunt Flo in the house?

Except it was *to* the house she was leading him—or rather, its replacement, the Dome. Perhaps she meant to skirt it—but no, right to the door. "Not in there!" The words were out before any thought had formed, like breath expelled by a blow to the stomach. He hardly remembered that entering the Dome was against the rules, the revulsion seemed more long-standing, directed against the structure's earlier incarnation, that Victorian monstrosity.

"Don't be so chicken," Jane said, inserting the key in the lock. "This is the safest place to talk. Everything has been set up for the Feast tomorrow, and until then it's off-limits—" she was having difficulty turning the key—"so no one is likely to come barging in."

She had it now. Pushed the door open. She paid no attention to Boone's mutter of protest. All she could hear was the loudness of her heartbeat. If there was a pornography of fear, this was it—the compulsion to look at its secret private parts.

"For crying out loud!" It was disappointment that dredged up the ejaculation from childhood. She stared with disgust at the familiar arrangement of tables duplicating that in the dining hut with the exception of white tablecloths and the more elaborate settings. "It looks like a banquet to be held at a Rotary Club."

What did she expect? Boone asked nervously, making sure the door was shut behind them. A banquet was a banquet, whether held under religious or commercial auspices.

Jane did not know what she had expected—certainly nothing so banal as this. Although the strings of colored lights had been removed, one festive touch from the party remained: the colored banners over the photographs. She was glad of that, having no wish to see those portraits again. But something had been added, she noticed belatedly. Beneath each banner was a wooden stand with the X-supports of a folding mechanism. And on each stand rested a roughly hewn wooden trencher. Just as the concealment of those photographs by bits of colored cloth only made them more intensely present, so did the emptiness of those trenchers nag her with the question of what they were meant to contain.

"Do you suppose," she asked Boone, drawing his attention to the stands, "they play some part in the taking of the Vow? Maybe they honor their departed spouses by placing little tidbits of the dinner before them?"

Boone shrugged. He did not care what their rituals were since he had no intention of playing any role but that of an observer. Automatically taking his accustomed seat at the end of one of the long tables, he began to unwrap his sandwich. Jane followed his lead and sat at the end of the opposing side, warning him not to disturb the settings and not to leave crumbs.

"That's what I want to talk to you about—I don't want to be an observer, I want to leave this place today, to hell with their feast." She looked across at him and felt a slight disorientation. He was not across from her. He was one seat down.

Boone grinned at her. "I was wondering when you'd notice that your side is short a setting. Obviously you're to sit it out in the barn while I am plied with sweetmeats and who knows what other enticements. You hate being shut out, I know, but that's no reason to spoil my fun. I promise to bring back a full report and even a few choice tidbits, if I can sneak them out."

It was with some satisfaction that Jane informed him the sweetmeats he anticipated would turn out to be a lowly stew. He made a face, which brought her to her senses. "What are we doing discussing the menu?" she exploded. "And it's not being shut out that bothers me, it's being shut in. As long as they thought they had one of us hooked—and one is all they want, they insist—everything was okay. But this morning, when you gave the game away and they knew you weren't converted either, it all changed. Something's up, Boone, and whatever it is, I don't like it."

Boone continued to chew his sandwich methodically. Between swallows he questioned her in that "reasonable" tone of voice that drove her wild. Exactly what did she think was up? Exactly what was she afraid of? Exactly what did she think they could do that would warrant creating a scene—and it would have to be quite a scene to get them to open the gates before the Feast of Elath was officially over? As if, Jane thought bitterly, her fear was nothing more than hysterical imaginings connected with her uterus. "We can't just walk out, we'd have to give them some reason for turning off the juice."

"Maybe we could turn it off. It's just a matter of pulling some switches, isn't it?"

"Simple," he agreed with his most deceptive wide-eyed look. "If you know where they are. Unfortunately, that's one of the things they have yet to show me."

"There you are," Jane said, "for all their open-handed hospitality, we've been kept on a pretty short lead. There's a hell of a lot we haven't been shown, it strikes me. And right now they're having a special meeting, very hush-hush, members only, but I bet they're making some rearrangements for the Feast tomorrow. You may be in for a surprise—all they have to do is switch your setting over to my side, and you will be the one sitting it out and I the one being plied."

At last she had gotten through to him. Red in the face, eyes bugging out, at a loss for words, he was semiphoring wildly. Surely an overreaction? "My God, you're choking!" she informed him and knocked her chair over in her haste to reach him, desperately trying to recall the details of that maneuver posted in restaurants. Pulling him up, she put her arms around him, placed her fists over what she hoped was the diaphragm and jerked hard. A bolus of bread popped out, landed neatly in the nearest bowl.

A reflex of coughing now seized him, but he was all right, all right, he croaked. What he wanted was water. A drink of water.

"The kitchen's over there," Jane said, remembering her earlier intrusion. It was from the center door under the mezzanine that Rafe had appeared, checking on the lights. Confidently she led him through the door into the kitchen. And what a kitchen—long and narrow and sheathed in stainless steel. The professional range, the double sink—each basin as large as a hip bath—even the cabinet doors and counter tops were of that cold polished metal. The only warmth emanated from an enormous butcher's block of unvarnished maple islanded in the center of the room. An institutional kitchen. Sleek and efficient, it left Jane cold.

Boone took a glass from an upper cabinet and drank thirstily. Jane found a roll of paper towels in a lower one and stood by to dry the water spots in the sink. Having made certain there remained no trace of their presence, she was about to follow Boone out. "Hey," she stopped him, "what do you suppose those are?"

Boone's gaze followed her pointing finger to the unbroken array of doors in the far wall, stainless steel set into stainless steel, unnoticeable except for the protruding handles and a small window in the center one.

He was sufficiently curious to walk over and stare in. "Humidity and temperature controlled for proper aging," he said, smacking his lips.

Over his shoulder, Jane saw the two goat carcasses, skinned and disemboweled, hanging from hook. Yuck, was her reaction. She preferred her meat cut up into unrecognizable sections. "And these?" she persisted, opening the adjacent door. A blast of air so cold it smoked persuaded her to close it quickly. A freezer with wire shelves, all empty. "All of these are freezers?" she asked incredulously.

Boone did not find it so unreasonable. "They grow a lot of vegetables in that garden, don't they? So they put a lot up for the winter. Freezing is better than canning, I would think."

"So where's the Birdseye stuff?" To answer her own question, Jane opened the next door.

On his way out, Boone was turned around by a strangled sound. "You sick or something?" he asked, noticing that her diaphragm was heaving. He could not see her face; her forehead was pressed against a closed freezer door, her hands spread on the metal as if she were being searched for a weapon by the police. He ran to catch her before she crumpled to the floor but she pulled herself out of his arms with a galvanic jerk. She seemed unable to speak—was she choking now?—but a trembling staccato of finger jabs commanded him to open the door. He opened it.

These shelves were filled. For a moment he was puzzled only by the rows of freezer-bagged melon-shaped objects. Then through the frost-clouded plastic he made out the eyes, the frozen nimbus of hair. The door slammed shut, he found himself pressing against the smooth steel even as Jane had done. For support, or to keep the horror in? He heard Jan retching in the sink. A contagious sound. By an effort of will he kept his own gorge from rising, steadied himself with several deep breaths before speaking.

"Let's get out of here," he said. To keep his voice from shaking, he had produced a flat monotone, drained of all affect. Jane had wiped her face with paper toweling, was now intent on stuffing it into her mouth. He led her into the banquet hall, pushed her into a chair, her pallor presaging a faint. He could neither sit nor stand still, the surge of fight-or-flight hormone coursing in his blood made him feel as if he were jumping out of his skin. Pacing behind her, he tried to ignore the heavy drumbeat inside his chest. He tried to think.

Staring in front of her, Jane saw nothing. Then bits of color impinged upon the blankness. Under those banners, the photographs of absent spouses, dimming even as the memory dimmed. But beneath them the wooden trenchers on which to place the grisly reminders. The departed ones are always with us, Rafe had said. With a shudder, she revised her flip retort: in spirit *and* in flesh. Now we are one, now we are one, now we are one, the Vow droned in her ear. But once we were two, would come from the trenchered heads encircling the diners, ice dripping from lashes like tears.

"We've got to make a break for it—but how do we get over that fence?" The question seemed drily academic, so low and controlled was Boone's voice.

"The stew—I know the recipe," Jane said and began to giggle. "Two parts goat and one part—" The giggles bubbled over into a crazy arpeggio of laughter.

Boone shook her, his hands digging into her shoulders until she cried out in pain. "That's better," he said. "Our only hope is to get out now while they're all at that meeting. There's one way I can think of—it may not work but we have to try it. If it doesn't—" his mouth twisted into something resembling a grin—"better fried than stewed, I always say."

To the machine shop, and run, don't walk, was all he stayed to tell her. Numbly she followed, close on his heels. Inside the Dome, surrounded by its intricate pattern of steel struts, she had felt half-dead, like an insect trapped in an upturned glass. With the open sky above her, she felt half-alive at least and the mere act of running seemed to promise escape.

To her surprise, Boone did not enter the shop but awaited her at the flank of the large machine outside. The one with the tall curving neck— the brontosaurus, he had dubbed it. Where were they going in that monster, she wondered, but did not question his order to get in. "We're in for it now," he said grimly, starting the motor. "They may not have seen us, but they sure as hell will hear us."

"I see what you mean," Jane shouted, her voice as well as her entire body vibrating as the old machine bumped across the uneven field. Boone did not answer. He was preoccupied with thanking God that what had no doubt been intended as make-work for him that morning had resulted in this antique harvester being ready to go. Jane looked back, saw the overalled, the calico-gowned figures spewing from the dining hut. A strangely familiar scene, echoing the moment of their arrival. And Rafe in the lead, hurrying to me, she thought but with quite a different emotion.

"Can't this damn thing go any faster?" she shouted, feeling an atavistic urge to beat the laboring machine, to kick it with her heels. "We'd do better on foot, it seems to me."

"You're wrong there," was all he said. He snatched a look at their pursuers, grimly headed toward the fence. Jane bit back a scream of warning—he knew as well as she what would happen if this hunk of metal they were riding in so much as touched it. Her held breath was expelled only when a wide swerve of the wheel turned them parallel to the fence. But the turn continued and now she did scream. "What are you doing? Are you going back to meet them?"

He braked to a full stop. "Get down," he ordered. "I've got to back this up, as close to the fence as I can get. You'll have to stop me before the rear end touches it or you know what will happen."

She nodded. Fried, instead of stewed. Quickly she scrambled down, understanding at last. Only this way would the tall blower with its crooked-neck spout extend over the fence. He put the machine into reverse, let it creep backward, his eyes glued to her waving hands. A cold sweat formed on her forehead as she recalled other times when he had trusted her eye for distance only to feel the impact of a bumper on bumper. Stop! she signaled. How much room was left? he demanded. She measured it with her hands: about a foot. He inched backward. Stop! she screamed.

This time he turned off the motor, swung himself out of the cab onto the machinery behind and hauled her up. She was to go first, all she had to do was to climb the spout, dangle from its end and drop to the ground on the other side of the fence. She embraced the metal tube, gripped it with her legs, he pushed, she slid back, he pushed, she slid back. She looked over her shoulder—another judgment of distance to make: how long before those overalled figures closed in on them. Rafe far in the lead, of course.

"I'll never make it," she said, drooping hopelessly against the metal tube she was embracing. "You go—quick, for God's sake—before they get both of us."

"Don't be an asshole," was his rough reply. "Get on my shoulders. And lift up your skirt—that stuff's too slippery."

With the head start he had provided, she was able to hoist herself forward . . . forward . . . "Good, let your body swing around and under. Hold on tight but let your legs go. Now drop!

She hit the ground, momentarily aware of a sharp pain. Scrambling to her feet, she cried out for Boone to hurry, hurry. What was he doing back in the cab, with Rafe almost on him? Why was he moving so slowly, so gingerly, as if he had all the time in the world, inching his way up the spout when surely he could jerk himself up faster? When at last he dropped down beside her and she leaned over to help him up, she could smell the fear in his sweat.

Run, run, her brain urged her but her muscles would not respond. No longer an avenue of escape, the spout had become the fatal flaw in Boone's plan—like a drawbridge left unraised. Another moment and Rafe would be up and over, and then the others. She was hardly aware of Boone dragging her along; like Lot's wife she had to look back, watch the final unfolding of her fate. Watch Rafe jump into the machine, land with a thud. Watch the infinitesimal shudder of the machine, the slow roll backward. Watch the crackle of sparks from the fence, the convulsive jerks of the body plastered to the spout. Smell the odor of acrid ozone and of burning flesh. A pillar of salt she had become, desiccated of all feeling.

Not once had Boone looked back. Leave the machine in reverse, on ground with a slight decline, a heavy-enough jar should do the rest. That had been his only hope. And his greatest fear while he still had to shinny up and over himself. "Let's get the hell out of here," he grunted now, content to leave Rafe's charred body an abstraction in his mind.

As they ran, he became aware of Jane's gait—half-hop, half-leap, as if she were competing in a sack race at a county fair. "Christ," he snarled, looking down at her ankle, "am I going to have to carry you?"

That he would, Jane had no doubt, but only Boone could perform a act of grace so gracelessly. There had been the same exasperation in his voice when he berated her for not knowing how to climb. My hero, she thought mockingly, but it was the mockery that did not ring true.

"I can manage," she said but he slowed down, insisted that she lean on him. They had a head start, he reassured her, someone would have to cut off the juice before the gate could be opened for any chase. And there ahead was the public road. They were bound to be picked up soon. Not soon enough, Jane feared, as they reached the Windigo sign. The wider road stretched ahead to a vanishing point, its emptiness as terrifying as any imagined throng of pursuers.

When they finally heard a car at their back, they were momentarily paralyzed. Belonging to the Society? If so, nowhere in this flat landscape to hide. If not, no time to lose, the car would soon speed by them. Of one accord, they moved into the middle of the road and turned to flag it down.

The large maroon sedan, of ancient vintage, slowed down, came to a stop with its eroded chrome bumper almost nudging their thighs. Complete strangers, the thin old man with a grey tuft of beard, the fat old woman at his side. Trouble? the old woman asked, sticking her head out the window. Oh, God, yes, Jane and Boone answered in unison.

"Please take us into town," Jane begged, moving quickly to the old woman's side, holding onto the door with a desperate grip. Although the woman seemed friendly enough (though somewhat weird with those cherry-red lips in an otherwise unmade-up face), Jane had no confidence in the philanthropy of the man, who kept his hand on the gear shift as if waiting for a traffic light to change, ready to shoot ahead.

"Look, it's the police we need," Boone said, sticking his head inside the car, aiming his words across the woman to the driver. "Just drop us off at the nearest station."

"Ask 'em where's their car. We ain't seen nothing on this road," the man said. Not looking at them, not even addressing them. A preemptory instruction to the woman who must be his wife.

Without waiting for the translation, Boone shouted, "There is no car, this is not a break-down. We've got to report a crime—"

"A horrible crime!" Jane shrieked, determined to breach the impassivity of the man, the complacent calmness of the woman.

"Tell 'em to get in, we ain't got all day." The man's grim trapdoor of a mouth hardly moved, only the bobbing of the grey tuft on his chin betrayed where the sound was coming from.

Jane and Boone did not wait for the message to be passed on. In the back seat they found themselves vying for room with two large garbage bags. From the woman in front a muffled apology for the untidiness back there—just some old clothes and things collected for the Volunteer Firemen's sale, squash them as much as they liked. "You come from that Society that took over old Sopher's farm?" From her tone, it was more the making of polite conversation than a question.

Boone's "Yes, but—" was blocked by Jane's "No, but—" Jane looked down at her dress, which must account for the know-it-all composure of this couple. Their passengers belonged to a strange religious cult—nothing would surprise them.

Boone leaned forward. "We're not members, we got stuck there because of this feast of theirs—"

Boone was disconcerted by the moon of a face thrust toward his. They were cheek to jowl—in fact, more than one jowl, and all quivering with smiles. A strong odor of cherry from that cherry-red mouth—she was sucking hard candy. "Everyone around here knows when they're having one of them feasts," she said. "You can hear that horn of theirs for miles around."

Maddened by Boone's penchant for the narrative form, Jane exploded. "They're cannibals! Cannibals, you hear?"

"I told you—one of them." the old man said, a remark no doubt intended only for his wife since he didn't ask her to pass it on.

The woman dug into a bag for another hard candy, remembered her manners and held the bag over her shoulder to those in the back. "Have one?" Boone was sufficiently stunned to put a hand out, but Jane knocked the bag aside, strafing them all with a cannonade of sourballs.

"What's with you people anyway? Are you all crazy? Maybe out here you eat each other all the time, maybe that's what makes you the backbone of this country, maybe that's what they mean by a vanishing way of life, the old verities that no longer hold. Only they're wrong, it's not vanishing, it's still going strong!"

Boone put his arm about her, squeezed tightly to still her shaking. "Calm down, calm down, it's the way you came out with it—of course they don't believe it—let me tell it my way."

She glared at him. "You make it sound like a joke and I stole your punch line."

"Look," he said, addressing the two in front, "I know this sounds incredible but let me tell you what we found out about this Feast of theirs—which occurs, the way I figure it, whenever a new couple comes along. For six days they have little feasts with the meat dish being goat, and then on the seventh—that's tomorrow, the biggie—" he swallowed hard, finding even the words indigestible—"they serve one of us to the other."

The two heads in front nodded at each other, a confirmation that he was meeting their expectations. A pick-up truck, loaded with feed sacks, passed them going the other way—the first traffic they had seen. The old man tooted his horn in greeting. His wife extruded her arm through the window as if signaling for a right turn, flapped a hello with her hand. "That's Al Jensen, a neighbor of yours," she said. "He thinks highly of what you folks have done with old Sopher's farm."

Boone pummeled the back of the woman's seat. Jane said bitterly it must be the way he told it. "Just take us to the police," he pleaded.

"Tell him to stop that," the old man snapped. "The springs are already coming through."

"Oh, we'll drop you off at the sheriff's," his wife translated, "but he ain't going to pay you any more mind than we do. It's not as if you're the first to come into town from that place screaming abut human heads kept in a freezer—"

Jane gasped. "You know about that? And nothing's been done to stop it?"

Indignantly the woman countered with the assertion that they had done what any God-fearing Christians would do: sent the sheriff, with every able-bodied man in town, armed to the teeth, ready for a shoot-out. "The second time, of course, he went over alone, kind of a duty call, I reckon, having a pretty good idea by then of what he'd find—"

"Which was what?" Boone asked, feeling as if all the air had been knocked out of him.

The woman sucked noisily at her sourball. "Goats' heads, of course," she said appreciatively. "Mister here seen them himself, being one of that first posse. Gave him a turn, it did, all them heads lined up on shelves, but there ain't no law against it."

Jane shuddered, seeing again the transparent freezer bags . . . frost coating the lashes, crystals of ice making a net of rhinestones for the hair. "Crazy," she moaned, "the whole thing's crazy." Not least the two people who had picked them up.

"Well, you know how it is with religions," the woman said tolerantly. "They all seem crazy except the one you've been brought up in. Now every Easter, I always fix a whole ham, with pineapple and cherries and brown sugar and mustard—"

"And the heads?" Boone interrupted the recipe. "How did they explain the heads, freezing them like that?"

"Now that was kind of sweet, I thought," the woman said, turning to smile at him. "It has something to do with showing respect for the animals they eat on these special occasions. You know, being vegetarians like they are, they probably feel guilty when they break the rule, want to show there're no hard feelings. Leastways that's the way I figure it."

Jane looked out the window, searching for some escape. A grain elevator, a sales office for farm machines—huge brightly painted combines displayed in front like a mechanized army massing for the attack—a water tower, half-obliterated railroad tracks. They must be approaching the town. All she hoped for now was quick release from the confines of this car. Still she could not help muttering, more to convince herself than this couple, "We *both* saw them. And we know a goat when we see one."

"Oh, I dunno," the woman tittered, "look at mister here, couldn't he fool you?"

Mister, as Jane saw in the rear-view mirror, appreciated the joke. The grey tuft on his chin wobbled up and down. Goatee. The word sprang unbidden into Jane's mind. He took his hand from the wheel and groped along the overflowing expanse of thigh, found the knee, squeezed it. With a coy slap, his wife rebuked him. "You old goat," she said fondly.

Maybe I *am* crazy, Jane thought. She was seeing herself in her wedding dress, the super's wife on her knees before her dispensing advice through the pins in her mouth: don't ever lose that tiny waist of hers. Had this woman been sent as a warning of what happened when you did?

Boone felt the futility of further words as much as she. In silence they entered what was obviously the town's main street, still retaining the width required by an earlier century's cattle drives, accommodating now the more leisurely activity of Saturday shopping. As if unwilling to be penned inside during such fine weather, the contents of the stores had spilled outside—sales racks of clothing, bins of hardware, sporting goods.

"Let us off here," Boone said abruptly as they passed under a banner that spanned the street. The American Legion, Post No. 142, was holding its annual barbecue.

Mister pulled up. Without shifting his gaze from the insect-splattered windshield, he said, "If they want the sheriff, they'd better look for him back of Legion Hall."

"That's where they're holding the barbecue," his wife explicated.

At least, Boone thought, he didn't go through his wife but spoke directly, if only to the road ahead. "Thanks," he said, to show he appreciated this growing intimacy. Jane followed him out of the car, winced with pain. Reminded of her turned ankle, he put a supporting arm around her waist.

"There, I knew it!" the woman cried, her face dimpling with amusement. "You're new-marrieds, ain't you, on your honeymoon?"

Boone and Jane exchanged an incredulous stare, then gave each other a little bob of acknowledgement, as at a formal introduction. Began to laugh, an emotion of last resort. The car pulled away. "Have a happy!" the fat woman shouted back at them.

"What are we laughing at?" Jane asked, abruptly sober.

"I've got an even better question—what do we do now?"

Jane equivocated, suggested the coffee shop across the street, where they could sit and sort things out. She took grim satisfaction in her forethought when Boone, brow furrowed in distress, turned out his pockets to signal their emptiness. The look he gave her when she slipped him his wallet was one of true devotion.

They walked into clammy darkness. The place had the cave-like ambience of a bar. Jane was relieved to see that the man at the counter was being served not the shot glass of whiskey she half-expected but a large slab of lemon pie, aquiver with mile-high meringue.

They chose a table at the care-curtained window, which allowed some daylight to slip through, and tried to ignore the look the approaching waitress gave them. One of *them*, she might as well have said. Ice tea, Boone ordered, and Jane the same although tempted by the lemon pie until she noticed how the buttocks of the man eating it overflowed the stool.

"So what *did* we see?" Boone asked, a terrible doubt in his eyes. He knew what she would answer, but did he want to hear it?

"I know what *I* saw," Jane said stubbornly, "and they weren't goats."

Boone took her hand—to comfort here? To be comforted? Whichever, it felt good. "So we go to the sheriff?"

Jane hesitated, came to a decision. "What's the point? They'll write us off as loonies, like the others. The main thing is that we're not."

"You mean everyone's crazy but thou and me, and sometimes I have my doubts about thee," he said with a grin., lighthearted with relief that no further action would be required of him.

"Oh, I've my doubts about thee too," she retorted, and looked down at her hands, gripped as for arm wrestling. Certainty, she thought wearily, came at too high a price.

For some time they sat there, sucking cold sweet tea through plastic straws, not knowing where they would go, what they would do. Both started to speak. Stopped. You go, Boone said politely. No, you, Jane said.

"Oh, it's nothing."

"It's nothing," Jane said too. But there eyes met, reflecting a different kind of terror, the possibility of happiness.